Blind Faith

Blind Faith

ELLEN WITTLINGER

Simon & Schuster Books for Young Readers
New York · London · Toronto · Sydney

1-4071

SIMON & SCHUSTER BOOKS FOR YOUNG READERS
An imprint of Simon & Schuster Children's Publishing Division
1230 Avenue of the Americas, New York, New York 10020

SIMON & SCHUSTER BOOKS FOR YOUNG READERS
is a trademark of Simon & Schuster, Inc.
Book design by Jessica Sonkin
The text for this book is set in Aldine401 BT.
Manufactured in the United States of America
2 4 6 8 10 9 7 5 3 1
Library of Congress Cataloging-in-Publication Data
Wittinger, Ellen.
Blind faith / Ellen Wittlinger.—1st ed.
p. cm.
Summary: While coping with her grandmother's sudden death and her
mother's resulting depression and fascination with a spiritualist church,
whose ministers claim to communicate with the dead, fifteen-year-old Liz
finds herself falling for a new neighbor whose mother is dying of cancer.
ISBN-13: 978-1-4169-0273-7
ISBN-10: 1-4169-0273-2
[1. Death—Fiction. 2. Spiritualists—Fiction. 3. Grief—Fiction.
4. Depression, Mental—Fiction. 5. Mothers and Daughters—Fiction.
6. Religion—Fiction. 7. Family life—Massachusetts—Fiction.
8. Massachusetts—Fiction.] I. Title.
PZ7. W7843B1 2006
[Fic]—dc22 2005008281

FIRST
EDITION

For Vanessa, who believes

ACKNOWLEDGMENTS

And with grateful thanks to my editor, David Gale; his assistant, Alexandra Cooper; my agent, Ginger Knowlton; and Pat Lowery Collins, Anita Riggio, and Nancy Werlin for their help and advice on the manuscript.

"If God did not exist, it would be necessary to invent him."
—VOLTAIRE

*"Parting is all we know of heaven,
And all we need of hell."*
—EMILY DICKINSON

Chapter One

The funeral was almost over. Mom and I had both gotten up from our front-row folding chairs to place single red roses on the casket as it hovered over the excavated hole in the earth. After days of thinking about nothing but this, I was grateful to finally feel a little numb. I flopped back down onto the chair next to my dad and stared at the granite headstone, which, along with my grandfather's name, Joseph McCoy, would soon be inscribed with my grandmother's: Elizabeth Kimball McCoy.

Really, it ought to just say "Bunny" on the headstone— that's what everybody called her. Even me. Elizabeth Kimball McCoy sounded like a woman who invited people over for tea and crossed her stockinged legs at the ankles. Bunny was black coffee to go—a jeans-and-sneakers kind of person. But if there was an opening at her gallery, she'd tie a silk scarf around her neck and wear earrings that dangled to her shoulders. Bunny was a person you noticed.

I'd just realized that my mother was still standing up, staring at her tossed rose, when she suddenly launched herself onto the casket, her arms outstretched to embrace the big silver bullet. A moaning sound turned within seconds to wailing.

"Oh, my God, I can't stand it! Don't leave me, Bunny! *You can't leave me!*" she screamed. The wind was blowing up the skirt of her hurriedly purchased, badly fitting black dress so that the backs of her pale thighs gleamed in the sun. I closed my eyes and pretended I was invisible.

Dad was on his feet immediately, grabbing her around the waist, pulling her off the casket lid.

"No, no! Don't take her away!" Mom yelled, sobbing, hitting at Dad's arm as if he were responsible for Bunny's burial. "I'm not ready!"

Dad stood there, holding her tightly until she slumped against him and the sobbing turned back into regular crying. That's the kind of thing he's good at—being there when you need him. He might not always know the right thing to say, but he's there.

I felt a single tear trickle down my cheek and calmly brushed it away. I was tired of crying. I wanted this funeral to be over already so we could all go home and try to figure out how to be normal people again, if that was possible.

I could hear mumbling behind me, and I turned halfway around in my seat to look at the other so-called mourners. There were people I didn't even recognize staring at Mom as if she had a third eye. Roxanne and her mother were in the back of the crowd, and they were looking at Mom too. Everybody seemed sort of embarrassed, which made me mad, even though I was totally humiliated myself. What did they expect? Didn't they understand how different everything was now? That nobody could ever take Bunny's place?

People always said how unusual it was that Mom and Bunny were so close, more like sisters or best friends than mother and daughter. *Christine and Bunny are so lucky,* they'd say. *I wish I had such a wonderful relationship with my mother!* Which always made me feel a little strange—like, how come I wasn't part of this chain of mother-daughter best friends too? But I just wasn't. Oh, Bunny loved me, that I knew for sure, but my mother—well, she was *certainly* not my best friend. Sometimes she didn't even act like my mother, at least not like most mothers. No *How was school today?* or *Let's go shopping together.* Bunny was the one who supplied me with that stuff. Dad always said Mom had her mind on other things because she was an artist. She was supposedly *thinking* all the time. Not about me, though. I guess Mom named me after her mother so I'd be like her, but I'm not. I'm just Liz. Nobody is like Bunny. Or rather, nobody *was.*

A few years ago Bunny took me shopping for back-to-school clothes at the end of the summer. We were at the mall in Waverly, and we kept running into girls I knew who were shopping with their mothers. I guess Bunny realized I was starting to feel kind of weird about that. We went to a restaurant for lunch and she ordered us both chocolate shakes.

"You know your mother loves you very much," Bunny said as I slurped my ice cream.

Did I know that? I wasn't sure.

Bunny sighed. "Perhaps it's my fault. After Joe died—your grandpa—Christine was so upset. She was only ten years old and I felt so sorry for her. I stood on my head to make her smile again. Gave her everything she wanted and more. Told her how special she was, day and night. I'm afraid it's made her a bit . . . self-centered."

I was in the kind of mood to think, *Why'd she even have a kid, then?*

Bunny always seemed to know what was on my mind. "When your mother was young, she always said she didn't want to marry and have children. All she wanted to do was throw pots. She was so focused on her art, she hardly had any friends. *I* dragged her to the concert where she met your father, and then I had to convince her she should take the time to get to know him.

"It opened her up, marrying your dad and having you, Elizabeth. She became part of a larger world, and I was so glad to see the change in her. But Christine is who she is," Bunny said, sighing. "Her passion is still there, the desire to lock herself away in her studio and ignore the rest of the world."

"Except for you," I said. "She lets *you* in."

Bunny reached across the table and took one of my hands in both of hers. "Oh, my darling girl," she said a little sadly. There was nothing else to say.

I'm not exaggerating when I say Bunny knew everybody in the Valley and they all liked her. So many people showed up at the wake at the Waverly Presbyterian Church that there wasn't room for all of them in the chapel and some had to sit on folding chairs in the rec hall next door. Artists from all over the Valley were there, and professors from the college, even a few people who'd known Bunny for all of her sixty-four years. All of them saying how shocked they were that Bunny, of all people, could have been so suddenly betrayed by her heart. I knew what they meant. Bunny had seemed too *alive* to die.

At first I was scared to look at Bunny lying in the coffin—I'd seen dead animals before but never a dead person—but once I got up the nerve to look, I was more amazed than freaked out. It looked just like Bunny, her long lashes lying against pink cheeks, her favorite rusty-brown lipstick carefully painted on her lips, her trimmed and polished fingernails resting on her chest, her turquoise scarf tied around her neck, one of its ends tucked beneath her long fluffy white hair.

Someone standing behind me said, "It looks like she's just asleep, doesn't it?" And then I realized what was so strange. I'd never *seen* Bunny asleep, never even seen her sitting quietly. Bunny had always been in motion: talking, pacing, driving, planning, working, on her way from one thing to another. Neither her lips nor her eyes were ever closed, and her hands were constantly busy helping to describe whatever it was she was talking about. Or they were pounding out jazz tunes on her big old piano. This wasn't Bunny lying here, it was only her left-behind body dressed up to look like her. In which case, where *was* she? How could it happen that the part of Bunny that was really *her* could just disappear?

The minister said a last prayer and finally people began to move away from the grave site toward their cars. Mom had gotten herself under control and was weeping quietly into the arm of Dad's jacket. Roxanne waved to me as she and her mother turned to go, and I raised my hand just a little to wave back. It seemed wrong even to wave, to do anything normal. Was everything going to be weird like this forever?

I stood next to Dad, wishing we were already back in the black limo, hidden away, but people were gathering around us again—friends, neighbors, teachers from the school where Dad was the principal, people I didn't even recognize—all saying the same things they'd been saying for days. No wonder Mom started screaming back there. I might have to scream myself if one more stranger pressed her squashy cheek into my face, saying, *sorry, sorry, sorry.*

Mom's friends Eva and Rosemarie kissed her quickly and said they were headed over to our house to put out food for anyone who came by after the service. Then several of Bunny's old friends came up and smothered us all in perfumed hugs, holding Mom the longest.

"She's in your heart, love. You'll never lose her," Claire said, patting Mom's hand. Which just made her cry harder.

"You call me if you need *anything,* dear. Understand?" said Lucille. Mom nodded, but I knew she'd never call Lucille, who some days couldn't even remember the names of her own cats.

I was shocked to see Mrs. Crosby, our neighbor from the ramshackle house across the road, waiting to talk to us. I halfway expected her to start complaining that our dogs had been in her yard again—we almost never spoke to her except when she yelled over from her front porch about keeping Pete and Woody out of her bedraggled flower beds. Roxanne and I had called her Mrs. Crabby since we were little. But now here she was pumping Dad's hand up and down and looking Mom right in the eye.

"Too bad about your mother dying. Death is hard, no two ways around it. If you'd like me to bring you over a cake, I'd certainly do that. I'm asking because I know sometimes you get too much of that junk after a funeral and half of it goes right down the garbage disposal."

Her little speech was at least successful in drying up Mom's tears. "Oh, well, thank you, Mrs. Crosby, for offering. You're right, several people have brought food by in the past few days. Please don't go to any trouble—we're being well taken care of."

Mrs. Crosby nodded. "Well, that's why I asked first. No sense wasting my time and ingredients. If you need anything, you know where to find me." She turned her back and walked off stiffly.

"God, she's weird," I said.

"Now, Lizzie," Dad said. "It was kind of her to make the offer."

I snorted as we began walking back to the car. "I'm glad we didn't have to waste her *ingredients*," I said, but quietly enough that Mom and Dad didn't hear.

A woman had been kind of hovering in the background while we talked to everybody else, but as we got near the car, she came up to us. She was older than Mom but not as old as Bunny, and she wore one of those long tie-dyed dresses you could get at the store in Waverly that Mom called "the shop for aging hippies." On her arms she wore about a hundred thin bracelets, which made a tinny noise when she moved. Her frizzy gray and brown hair was tied back carelessly with a string of yarn.

"You don't know me," she said. "My name is Monica Winters and I was one of Bunny's biggest fans. I live out in Bishop's Hill. Bunny gave me an exhibit in her gallery a few months ago—I'm a printmaker—and she's been visiting me regularly all year. I just wanted to say, she was a wonderful woman. You're very lucky to be her daughter."

Mom was wiping her face with one of Dad's already sopping-wet handkerchiefs. She handed it absentmindedly to me, and I gave the thing back to him. Mom just stared at the woman as though she were too exhausted to make sense of her words.

"Thank you," Dad said finally, speaking for her. "We appreciate that." We started to walk away, but this Monica person stepped in front of Mom again.

"And . . . I just wanted to say that if you ever want to try to get in touch with Bunny . . . well, I belong to the Spiritualist Church up at Singing Creek. . . . I don't know if you're familiar with it, but we . . . our preachers are mediums and they could try to contact her for you. I'm not trying to be pushy or anything, but . . ."

Mediums? Like at a *seance*? What was she talking about?

"Thank you," Dad said again, this time more forcefully. "I think we need to be getting home now."

"Of course," Monica said, stepping aside. "I just wanted to let you know about it. Bunny was such a strong person in life, I just know she'd want to reach out to you from the Other Side!"

Mom and I kept looking at Monica as Dad hustled us into the waiting car. Mom had stopped crying. I kind of wished I could ask Monica a few questions. Like, do you really believe you can talk to dead people?

Obviously Mom was wondering the same thing. "Do you think they could really contact Bunny?" she asked Dad.

"There's a *church* where they do that?" I said.

Dad shook his head. "She's some kind of a kook, that's all. This is the first time I've heard of a religious nut trying to recruit people at a funeral." He settled himself next to me and pulled the door closed.

As the driver began the slow circle out of the cemetery, I looked back again. Monica was sitting down on one of the folding chairs next to Bunny's grave. She seemed to be talking to someone, except there was no one else there.

Chapter Two

*I*n the three weeks after Bunny's funeral my mother didn't work in her studio at all; in fact, most days she barely got out of bed. She refused meals, saying she wasn't hungry, but sometimes she came floating downstairs in a long nightgown to eat a handful of crackers or make herself a cup of tea.

Her friends Eva and Rosemarie called every day at first. They tried to get her to have lunch with them or go to a movie, but she told them she was too tired, she just needed to rest. One day they came over and tried to force her to get dressed and leave the house with them. They started out joking and laughing, but when Mom refused to crack a smile or even take the eyeshade off her eyes, they lost their sense of humor pretty quickly. After that I guess they gave up. Mom said she was glad they'd stopped "pestering" her.

But I think the thing that freaked me out the most was that she didn't seem to be brushing her hair anymore—or even washing it. It hung in clumps that she didn't bother to push back out of her eyes. For the first time ever she looked . . . old. Which made me feel kind of sick to my stomach. My mother has always been very proud of her long dark hair, and although she has to tie it back when she works in the pottery studio, the rest of the time it swings around her face like a velvet curtain. I always wanted my hair to do that too, but I'd gotten Dad's hair, reddish and curly. I wore it long, but it didn't swing; it flew. I was forever trying to find clips and barrettes that would keep it tamed. But now Mom's hair looked worse than mine— birds could have been nesting in that mess and you wouldn't even have known it.

It was a good thing that school was over for the year. Between Bunny's death and Mom's reaction to it, I was too distracted to do much studying. I didn't do as well on my exams as I should have, but I got As in my classes anyway. I'm one of those kids who teachers just expect to do well, so I can slip up once in a while without them paying too much attention to it. Which I know is highly annoying to kids who work hard for every A they get, or kids like Roxanne, who'd decided getting As wasn't worth the effort she had to put into it.

The downside to school being over for the year was that I couldn't use the piano at the high school to practice anymore, and every time I played my keyboard at home, Mom would whine at me. "Please stop that, Liz. I need to sleep!" As if she hadn't been sleeping for *days* already. I needed to practice if I was going to be ready for my recital.

One afternoon I'd gone into her room with a wastebasket to pick up the pile of used tissues that was growing into a good-size hill next to her side of the bed. But when she saw what I was doing, she yelled at me to go away and leave her be. "I want to look at all my tears," she said. Which made me shiver.

I kept waiting for Dad to do something to make Mom start acting normal again. One afternoon I heard him talking to her in their bedroom.

"I wish you'd come downstairs for dinner tonight. I'm making chicken breasts the way you like them, with white wine and olives."

"Jack, I told you, I can't eat. My stomach is too upset," she said.

"How about if you just come down and sit with us, then," he suggested. "I think it would make Liz feel better."

"Well, it wouldn't make *me* feel better," she said. "I'm sorry, Jack. You and Liz will just have to do without me for a while."

Later I asked Dad when he thought Mom would start to feel better. All he said was, "Give her time, Liz, give her time." How much time did she need? I missed Bunny too, and I was sure I would always miss her. But you get tired of crying after a while—you have to get back into your life. And I didn't think lying in bed all day was making Mom feel any better.

Dad has always done most of the cooking for us, anyway—he enjoys it—so that was no different, but sitting alone at the kitchen table with him every evening made me feel that Bunny's death really had changed everything forever. Not only had I lost Bunny, I'd lost Mom, too. I wasn't sure which was worse.

It was especially strange to go into Mom's quiet studio. Normally, the radio would be tuned to some NPR station where people were arguing about the war in Iraq or AIDS in Africa or public education in America. And the pottery wheel would be spinning around, or maybe Mom would be wedging clay, or she and Bunny would be discussing glazes. The kiln might be firing, which would make the whole big room warm and cozy. But now it was as if the studio had been put to sleep. Mom's unfinished pots had been covered with plastic right after Bunny died, and they stood that way still. Eventually they would dry out if she didn't come back to finish them. The kiln was open but hadn't even been unloaded after the last firing. The shade was pulled down over the shop entrance and the sign that said POTTERY STUDIO OPEN leaned against the inside of the door. Even though the studio had always seemed like *their* world and not mine, it depressed me to see it like this, as dead as Bunny.

Roxanne came over one Saturday a few weeks after the

funeral. The spring mud had finally dried up and we planned to do our annual beginning-of-summer hike up Goat Mountain. It was an easy hike, although the first year we'd done it, when we were about ten, it had seemed like a big adventure. By the time we were twelve or thirteen, we'd hike up a couple times a week. We had some secret hiding spots where we left stuff from day to day—special trinkets and games and journals. But last year we only went up once, and I was pretty sure this year would be the same. Roxanne had a boyfriend now, Paul, and he liked her to spend most of her time with him. So Roxy and I had to make plans if we wanted to spend time together. It didn't just *happen* anymore.

I made tuna sandwiches, because we always took tuna sandwiches up Goat Mountain. I packed my backpack with those plus fruit and granola bars and cream soda—that was the tradition. Roxanne would bring magazines and MadLibs and a deck of cards, because that's what she always brought. I was glad that at least this one thing wasn't going to change.

I hadn't spent any time with Roxanne since right after Bunny's funeral, when she and her mom had come by the house. Roxy was working and I was busy too, but it wasn't just that. I didn't want Roxy, or anybody, inside my house in case Mom was wandering around barefooted with that blank look on her face, as if she didn't know where she was anymore. I didn't know how to explain it.

But, of course, Roxanne noticed everything. We were barely out of my front yard when she said, "Is your mom still depressed about Bunny's death?"

"What do you mean?" I was stalling.

"Well, usually on Saturdays she puts out the sign that her studio is open. It's getting warm; there could be tourists driving by."

I shrugged. "She'll probably do it next weekend."

"Plus," Roxanne said, "when I came up the road, I saw her standing by her bedroom window, kind of staring out. It looked like she was wearing a bathrobe."

I sighed. "She does that a lot lately. The staring thing. And the bathrobe." We were across the road by then and onto the path by the stream that heads up The Goat, so I bent down to take the leashes off of Pete and Woody. They ran circles around us, they were so happy. "These guys have been begging me for a hike," I said. "Remember that time we took them all the way to Carson River?"

Roxanne was not easily sidetracked. "I guess anybody would be sad if their mother died. And Bunny was very cool for a grandmother. But, I mean, your mom is a grown-up."

"Mom and Bunny were best friends!" I yelled louder than I meant to. "Just imagine if your mother *and* your best friend died." Since Roxy was *my* best friend—or used to be, anyway, before Paul—it made my heart thud to think about what I'd just said.

"I know, but she can't stay up in her room forever."

"She's not staying in her room *forever*," I said. "She's just . . . resting. She'll be better pretty soon." Would she? I hoped I was right about that.

"It's funny," Roxy said. "When my grandmother died, it didn't seem like a big deal at all. I mean, we flew to Ohio for the funeral, and it was sad while it was going on, but not *that* sad. And then afterward we ate dinner at Red Lobster and that was that."

That sounded about right for Roxanne's family. None of them seemed to like each other all that much, including her parents.

"I don't think that's normal, Roxanne," I said.

"What's *normal*?" she said. "Adults are all just weird in different ways."

I smiled. Roxy might not get As, but she had a way of understanding people that was always interesting. It was one of the things I missed now that we didn't see each other as much.

We'd reached a steep part of the climb, and we stopped talking for a while. But my brain wasn't quiet. It had gotten stuck on a picture of Bunny striding around the big barnlike studio, admiring Mom's new work—not just the plates and vases the tourists bought, but her more complicated stuff, the free-form sculptures that Bunny showed in her gallery. Bunny was gulping coffee as the two of them discussed form, design, balance—stuff about art that I never really understood.

The minute I walked into the house I could tell if Bunny was there—the air would be charged with her energy. Even if Bunny left before I got home from school, I could tell she'd been there. Mom would be working feverishly at her pottery wheel, whistling a Patsy Cline tune, or mixing glazes at the bench and singing folk songs at the top of her lungs. Just being around Bunny made you feel so alive you wanted to get up and *do* something.

Roxy and I got to the top of The Goat in about an hour. She spread out a blanket in our favorite spot while I poured water into a bowl I'd brought along for the dogs. Then we both lay back to feel the sun on our faces. As soon as I unwrapped a sandwich, the dogs smelled the food and came over to see what they were missing. Woody, the yellow Lab, had managed to get his feet wet, and he muddied my sleeve, pawing me and begging for a bite.

"Woody!" I said, sitting up. "Stop it!" He looked at me soulfully until I broke off some of my sandwich and fed it to him.

Pete was less well behaved. "Hey!" Roxanne shouted. "Pete got a granola bar!" The scrawny mutt was trotting away with his treasure, eating wrapper and all.

"Guard the one that's left," I said. "We'll share it."

Roxanne reached over and pulled off a branch of grapes. "Do you think your mom will come to your recital next week?" she asked.

"Of course she will," I said, although I'd been worrying about it myself.

Roxy leaned her head on her elbow and looked at me. "I mean, you've been practicing so much and you're really good. She ought to come."

"Roxanne, she *will*!" I couldn't discuss this with Roxy anymore, it made me too nervous. So, I changed the subject to one I knew she'd appreciate. "What's Paul doing today? Or does he just stay home and weep when he can't be with you?"

"Yeah, right. He's playing basketball with his boys."

"Will and Dan and those guys?"

"Yeah. You know Paul. He's got a million friends."

So did Roxanne, now. Paul had introduced her to all of his friends and she fit right in with them. I was a little jealous, I'll admit, but I wouldn't have been comfortable hanging around with a big group like that, where you felt like you always had to say something funny or cool. Roxy could do it, but I'd just blush and mumble and feel stupid. So, I tended to stay home alone, practicing the piano and feeling like a big loser.

The whole idea of boys being people you would actually *choose* to spend time with was pretty much totally incomprehensible to me. I could never think of anything to say to them, and they seemed equally dumbstruck by my presence. I think Roxy was right when she told me, "Getting straight As is not exactly an aphrodisiac." Once they grew up, like Dad, males apparently became human again, but the younger ones were aliens. All that loud talking and pounding on each other—it was embarrassing how much they wanted attention. I mean, I was attracted to men in movies, like Johnny Depp or Orlando Bloom, but I couldn't imagine having a boyfriend I'd have to actually *speak* to.

"Paul's coming to your recital with me on Friday," Roxy announced between bites of tuna fish.

"He is? Why?"

"Because I asked him to. Maybe we could get some of his other friends to come too. Dan broke up with Melanie, you know. Maybe if he came—"

"No! *Please*, Roxanne! I'm nervous enough as it is. I don't want you bringing some boy with you who thinks . . . whatever he thinks. I don't even want Paul to come."

"For God's sake, Liz! What difference does it make who's sitting in the audience? You won't even know—"

"I'll know if you tell me!"

Roxy sighed. "Okay, I won't tell you."

"And don't bring anybody either. Okay?"

"I can't tell you."

"Roxanne!"

"Okay! I'll come by myself. Geez, I'm surprised you're allowing *anybody* to come."

"Believe me, I wouldn't if Mr. Bellerose wasn't making me. He says I have to get used to playing before an audience. I have to learn to handle my nerves."

"Well, he's right about that."

"Why? I'm not going to be a concert pianist or anything. I just like playing the piano for myself."

"But you're really good. Don't you want people to know how good you are?"

I shrugged. "What difference does it make?"

Roxanne shook her head. "Sometimes I really don't get you, Liz. You work so hard at everything, but you don't even seem proud of yourself. If I could play piano like you can or write as well as you can or . . ."

I brushed her compliments away. "I'm not really that good. It just seems that way because nobody else in Tobias is very good either. If I lived in a city, they wouldn't even *allow* me to give a recital."

Roxy's face clouded over. "Now you're really pissing me off. If *you're* not good at the piano or writing or anything, what does that make me? A total failure?"

"No, that's not—"

"Well then, stop putting yourself down all the time. It's getting really annoying."

I could tell she meant it. "Okay, I'm sorry."

We didn't talk for a few minutes. Then Roxy pulled the deck of cards out of her backpack and we made room on the blanket to play twenty or thirty rounds of Bullshit.

Roxanne stowed the leftovers in our backpacks while I rounded up the dogs. The two of them had found a big stick and didn't want to give up tussling over it. I managed to get it away from them and carried it down The Goat so they could play with it in our yard.

When we got back, Dad was raking leaves off the flower beds around the porch. I was surprised to see him doing yard work—that was usually Mom's job. Of course, you had to get out of bed to rake leaves. Usually Dad played tennis on the weekends with friends or teachers from his school. Or sometimes he'd go hiking or take a bike ride. On Sundays, if Mom and I went to church with Bunny, Dad stayed home and read books. "I'll get my wisdom from Tolstoy rather than the Gospels," he'd say. "I trust Leo over Peter and Paul any day."

On a normal early-summer weekend he'd have bribed me or paid a neighborhood kid to do whatever outdoor chores Mom hadn't done. But that Saturday he was wearing an old T-shirt and scraping up last fall's remaining leaves himself. "I just realized there were actually plants coming up under here," he said. "Thought I ought to give them a fighting chance." His smile looked forced.

"Want us to help?" I asked.

"I wouldn't mind, but there's only one other rake."

"You rake," Roxanne said, never one to volunteer for work. "I'll throw the stick for Pete and Woody." The dogs were already leaping crazily to try to get it from where she was swinging it over her head.

We worked for twenty minutes or so, uncovering

hollyhocks and daisies. Seeing the green plants pushing up from under the dead leaves made me remember what they'd look like in a few weeks, tall and blooming, bending in the breeze as always. It made me feel a little optimistic— not *everything* had died with Bunny.

"One more time. My arm is getting tired," Roxanne told the dogs, and then pitched the stick farther than she had before, right across the street and onto Mrs. Crosby's front porch.

"Oh, no!" Roxanne cried. "It's in *her* yard!"

Both animals raced across the street, as Dad and I tried to call them back. The street was not a heavily traveled one, and there were no cars coming, thank God, but I knew Mrs. Crosby would have a hissy fit if she saw the dogs on her property.

Which she did. Her screen door banged open before they even reached the stick. Did Mrs. Crosby sit behind her curtains and *wait* for people to make mistakes? She bent down, picked up the stick, and cracked it over her knee— not once but three times. The small sections were no longer of interest to Woody and Pete who had stopped dead in their tracks to watch her.

Mrs. Crosby lifted her saggy arm and pointed at me. "You, Girl!" she yelled at me. "Didn't I ask you nicely to keep these durn mongrels in your own yard? They wreck my flowers! And I don't relish picking up dog poop either!"

Nicely? Mrs. Crosby had never done a nice thing in her

life. I checked for cars and then called the dogs again. They ran back across the road, the stick already forgotten. Behind me I heard another screen door slam. I glanced over my shoulder and then, unbelieving, turned to stare. It was Mom, dressed in her good linen jacket, sunglasses covering her reddened eyes, her hair bushy but brushed, a wobbly smile on her face and car keys in her hand.

"Hello, Mrs. Crosby! I'm so sorry!" she called over. "We'll try harder to keep the dogs over here. If there's ever any poop in your yard, call us and we'll come over and remove it."

"I'll do that," Mrs. Crosby said, then threw the pieces of stick over the porch railing. "I'm expecting company today and I'd like the place to look its best," she said, then disappeared back into her house. I would have been shocked that somebody was visiting Mrs. Crosby if I hadn't already been so shocked that Mom was out of bed and dressed.

"Chris, you . . . you look great," Dad said, putting a hand on her shoulder.

"Hi, Mom," I said, feeling almost shy. Her transformation from nightgowned ghost to friendly neighbor had happened too quickly. None of us knew how to react.

"Hi, Mrs. Scattergood," Roxanne said. "I guess you're feeling better."

"Yes, I am, Roxy. Thank you. I'm going out for a few hours, Jack. You don't mind, do you?"

"Of course not, but . . . where are you going?" Dad looked as confused as I felt.

"To church, actually." She lifted her chin as though she were proud of herself.

"It's Saturday afternoon," I said.

"I know. That's when they meet."

"That's when *who* meets?" Dad asked.

"The Spiritualists. Monica Winters called to see if I wanted to go to Singing Creek with her. We're going to contact Bunny."

Chapter Three

Roxanne acted like she knew all about the Singing Creek Spiritualist Church, which, of course, she didn't. As we walked to her house, she couldn't shut up about it.

"It's *creepy*." She shivered. "They pretend they see people who're dead, and they go into trances and scream and fall down! You'd never catch me in a place like that—talking to ghosts!"

"Who told you that?"

"I've heard about it!"

"It can't be that stupid. My mother wouldn't go to a place like that. Can you see her falling on the floor in her good linen jacket? I don't think so."

"If she really wants to talk to Bunny, she might."

I shook my head, trying to rid myself of the image of my

mother writhing on the dusty floor of some cuckoo cathedral. "Roxy, you always get scared by supernatural stuff. Remember when Noella Pace got that Ouija board for her birthday and you were afraid to even touch it?"

Roxanne pouted. "That was ages ago. We were just kids then. Besides, you got scared too after it told you how old you were, and what year you were going to die!"

"That was a dumb thing to ask it. That was Noella's idea."

"It said you were going to live to be eighty-five or something. I don't see why that was so scary."

"Because, nobody wants to think they're *ever* going to die! Would you want to know when you were going to die?"

"Yeah, if it was a million years from now, like yours was, I'd want to know that."

I gave up. Roxanne enjoyed arguing more than I did.

"What do you want to do when we get to my house?" Roxanne said. "Oh, I know! Paul and I went to the mall yesterday and I got some new makeup—a cream blush— and this gorgeous burgundy eyeshadow and matching nail polish. We could make each other up!"

I really didn't understand why Roxanne enjoyed makeup so much. She was pretty enough without it. I never liked wearing it: I blushed quite easily without any help, thank you, and why would I want to attract attention to my bitten-down nails?

"I really should go home and practice for a while," I said.

"Oh!" Roxanne was disappointed. "It's Saturday! Do

you really have to practice today? You're supposed to relax on the weekend."

I wrinkled up my nose. "I want to be perfect on Friday night. Besides, I like practicing."

Roxanne snorted. "You're the only kid I ever met who likes practicing the piano. Or any other instrument."

I shrugged. "Well, I do. Besides, now that I have Bunny's piano to play on instead of just a keyboard, it's really fun." The piano movers had come just the day before, carefully wedging Bunny's old upright through the front door and settling it in the dining room under one of Bunny's still-life paintings. Lots of her stuff had been squeezed into our house in the past three weeks. As each item was carried in, Mom started crying again, but I was glad to have all the reminders of Bunny around, as if she were still, somehow, with me.

I said good-bye to Roxanne and started walking back home. I was truly anxious to start practicing on the big piano—the sound was so much fuller than I could ever get with my keyboard—but it made me feel a little guilty to be so happy about it. After all, I wouldn't have it if Bunny hadn't died. And no piano on earth was worth that. Still, I loved that Bunny had written down specifically that *I* was to get her piano. Not Mom—*me*. Of course, Mom couldn't even play the piano, but still.

As I got closer to home, I noticed a pickup truck piled with furniture parked out in front of Mrs. Crosby's house.

Two men seemed to be carrying things inside. Or no, maybe one of the men was just a tall boy. This must be Mrs. Crosby's "company," but who were these people? Mrs. Crabby never even had visitors, much less anybody moving things into her house as if they planned on staying for a while.

I was so fascinated by the idea of anybody moving into Mrs. Crosby's house that I forgot about going inside to practice. I sat on my front porch steps between the dogs and brushed handfuls of hair out of their coats as I watched. There were some mattresses in the truck and two bureaus. Half a dozen suitcases and some boxes. A big plant. The boy carried in a guitar case and a boom box. I figured those were probably his, which must mean he was staying. Then a girl came running out the front door and said something to him. She seemed quite a bit younger than the boy, who was at least my age, maybe older. I couldn't figure it out. Was Mrs. Crosby renting out rooms? If so, she must not have known the people had kids. They wouldn't last long.

The girl looked over at me and waved, then called "Hi!"

Which made me feel incredibly stupid for sitting there obviously staring at them. I waved back and turned my attention to Woody, as though I was really only grooming my dog, not being nosy.

The girl dashed out into the street and headed straight for me. "Be careful, Courtney!" the boy yelled at her. "Did you even look for cars?" He sounded furious.

"I *looked*!" she said, although I knew she hadn't. This

was the second time today I was glad our street wasn't busy.

"Hi!" she called again as she sped up the lawn toward me. "Do you live here? My name's Courtney Arnold! What's your name? Are these your dogs?"

Woody and Pete jumped up and greeted her, wagging happily when she let them lick her face.

She was adorable, with huge dark eyes and stringy blond hair flying around her shoulders—maybe eight or nine years old. Her toenails had been painted blue, but the polish had chipped off, leaving her with polka-dot toes sticking out of her pink sandals.

"I'm Liz Scattergood," I said. "And these are my dogs, Woody and Pete."

"Cool," Courtney said. "We're gonna live across the street from you!"

"You are? With Mrs. Crosby?" It couldn't be true.

But the girl nodded. She was petting Woody so vigorously that clouds of dog hair floated up and caught on her T-shirt. "She's our grandma. Only we never saw her until now. 'Cause my mom was mad at her."

That was a new one on me. "Really? I didn't even know Mrs. Crosby *had* any children."

Courtney picked at a Band-Aid on her elbow. "Just my mom is the only one. And they didn't hardly talk for a long time. Except for now my mom is sick and, um, she called my grandma, and she said we could come here to stay for a while. Until my mom gets better."

I didn't know what to say. "Well, that was nice of her."

Courtney nodded. "Yeah, I think she's going to like us pretty much."

That, I thought, *would be the day.*

"Courtney!" The boy was coming up the lawn now too. "You're supposed to be helping me unpack stuff."

The girl sighed. "This is my brother, Nathan. He thinks he's my boss now just because Mom is sick."

"Courtney! God, you don't need to tell everybody our whole life story."

"I can say what I want." Courtney crossed her arms and glared at him. "Besides, I'm not telling everybody. I'm just telling Liz. She's our new neighbor."

Nathan looked embarrassed. "Sorry if she was bugging you," he said, but he didn't sound sorry in the least—anger was the only tone his voice seemed able to register.

"She wasn't." I smiled at Courtney.

"Her name is Liz Scaren . . . getti, or something," Courtney told Nathan.

"Scattergood," I said, laughing. I liked this kid already. She was sweet and funny and stood up for herself with her grumpy brother. I wished, not for the first time, that I had a sister. I hoped Courtney wouldn't get evicted from Mrs. Crosby's too quickly.

Normally, I wouldn't have been able to talk to a boy I didn't know, but having Courtney there made the situation easier. And the fact that he wouldn't really look at me helped too. "Courtney says you're going to live with Mrs. Crosby for a while," I said.

Nathan shrugged. "I guess so. Unless she kicks us out."

"Isn't she your grandmother?" I asked, as though grandmotherhood would turn Mrs. Crabby into a kind and generous old lady.

He grunted deep in his throat. "Yeah, since last week. Before that I didn't even know I *had* a grandmother. She probably didn't know she had us, either. It doesn't seem like she's all that thrilled about us showing up."

"Besides," Courtney said, "Mom says Grandma kicked *her* out one time."

"Courtney, will you *shut up*?" Nathan glared at her.

I wasn't surprised. Wouldn't you know the hag couldn't even get along with her own daughter?

"So your mother's been sick?"

Courtney nodded. "She's getting better, though. Grandma's gonna help her."

"That's great," I said, hoping for her sake it was true. "I guess that's your dad unloading the truck."

"Oh, no, that's Mr. Prescott, our old neighbor. He's just helping us out. Our dad isn't—"

Nathan grabbed her arm, interrupting her. "Courtney, I just remembered. Mom wanted you to bring that small makeup case in to her. She was going to paint your fingernails or something."

"Oh, yeah!" she said, jumping in the air. "Is it still in the truck?" She was running down the lawn already, her enthusiasm for nail polish stronger than her interest in me.

"Look for cars before you cross the street!" Nathan yelled to her, but she was already across and climbing into the back of the truck. "Dammit!" He kicked his heel into the grass so hard a little chunk of dirt flew up behind him.

"I like your sister," I said, a little freaked out to be suddenly alone with this angry guy.

He looked up at me, and I saw that he had the same big dark eyes as his sister, only his had no glint, no spark in them like hers did. His face closed down into a knot. "Look, I might as well tell you before you hear it someplace else—I know how neighbors gossip. My mother is dying. She has leukemia and she came here to die. But Courtney doesn't know yet, so please don't say anything to her. Okay?"

I stared at him, horrified. "Oh, God! No, of course I won't say anything."

He spit the words out of his mouth as if they were bad food. "My mom wants to tell Courtney herself. Like she told me."

"Oh. I'm really sorry, I'm *so* sorry about . . ."

But Nathan had already pivoted on his sneakers and was stalking away from me, away from my sorriness. And I knew why. Most likely he'd heard people's sympathies and regrets a hundred times already, and it hadn't helped one bit. His mother was going to die anyway, just like Bunny had, no matter how sorry anybody was.

Chapter Four

Dad was making his famous Saturday-night homemade pizza with mushrooms, olives, and three kinds of cheese when we heard car doors slam and two excited female voices approaching the back door. Mom was back, and Monica was with her.

Dad looked out the window over the sink and swore very quietly. Which was the only way he ever swore, as if he were talking to himself.

When Monica and Mom walked in the door, smiling and talking, I couldn't believe it. Mom actually seemed happy. I'd been thinking I might never see her smile again, and here she was, obviously in a very good mood.

She patted the top of my head absentmindedly and whipped off her sunglasses as she rushed in. "Oh good,

Jack's making pizza! I invited Monica to stay for dinner. There's enough to go around, isn't there?"

"I don't want to be any bother," Monica said, taking off the sun visor she'd been using to squash down her mane of hair.

Dad smiled at her, but it wasn't his usual big smile, just a half-baked one. "No problem. My pizza can feed any number. I just pile on more mushrooms."

"Like the loaves and fishes," Monica said.

I knew what she was talking about, even though I'd managed to avoid Sunday school most of the time. I remembered the story about Jesus and the small number of loaves and fishes that magically multiplied to feed a whole crowd of people. Bunny had read me a book of these stories—parables they were called—when I was little. They weren't to be taken as strict truth, she'd explained, but as metaphors for God's love. Stories to help you understand the meaning of God. I was never sure I really got the metaphors, but I liked the stories anyway.

Dad was quiet. He never liked it when people talked about church or religion. I'd once heard him tell Mom that religion was superstition on one side and hypocrisy on the other. He didn't believe any of it and he didn't trust people who did.

It was obvious to me that he didn't trust Monica, but Mom was too delirious to realize it. She poured glasses of wine for the three of them and settled herself and Monica at the kitchen table to relate the story of their afternoon while the pizza baked.

"You would *not* believe Singing Creek, Jack," she said.

"No, I'm sure I wouldn't." He busied himself tearing up lettuce leaves. "Lizzie, will you cut up an avocado for me?" he asked, handing it to me.

"Does it look like a regular church?" I asked. "I mean, like Waverly Presbyterian?" It occurred to me that that was the only church I'd ever been inside.

"No, the Presbyterian is much larger. Singing Creek is a small building with a few pews in an upstairs room. No stained glass windows or organs or steeples or Bibles."

"Some people bring their own Bibles," Monica said. "And we have hymnbooks and a piano."

"Yes, we sang a few songs," Mom said. "The service begins with healings. The way it works is, the healers stand—"

But I wasn't interested in all the details—I wanted to get to the point. "Did you talk to Bunny?"

Mom smiled at Monica as though they had a secret between them.

"She was there," Monica said. "I could feel her."

Dad tossed silverware onto the table without caring too much where it landed. "*You* did? I didn't know *you* were a medium."

"Monica goes to a psychic development group," Mom said. "Led by Running Fox, one of the preachers at Singing Creek."

"*Running Fox?*" Dad shook his head. "This area is lousy with those old hippie types."

Mom glanced at Monica, a little embarrassed probably, since Monica looked like a Woodstock refugee herself. "His real name is Peter Noble," Mom said. "He used to be a lawyer, but he stopped practicing so he could devote all his time to Spiritualism. His spirit communicator is Gray Fox, so when Reverend Peter is channeling him, he calls himself Running Fox."

Dad shook his head but didn't comment.

I was getting impatient; the avocado had been sliced and my question remained unanswered. "But did Bunny *say* anything to you? Isn't that why you went there? So she'd talk to you?"

Mom sighed and leaned her head back to look up at the ceiling. "I think she was there. I really do."

"Why?" I wanted to know. "What happened?"

"I didn't say a *thing* to Reverend Irene beforehand," Monica said. "When I called you this afternoon, I didn't even think you'd come with me."

"Who's Reverend Irene?" Dad asked.

"What did Bunny *say*?" I demanded.

Mom put up her hand to stop our questions. "Reverend Irene is one of the three Spiritualist ministers at Singing Creek. She did my reading—that's what they call it. First she asked me if she could 'come to me.' That's a standard question, Monica says. Then you have to say something like, 'Yes, you may,' so they hear your voice, and then they tell you what they see or hear or feel from . . . the spirit world." She stopped and looked at Monica. "I'm not crazy, am I?"

Dad grunted, but Monica leaned over and laid a hand on Mom's knee. "Absolutely not. I know at first it's hard to believe, but the more you come to Singing Creek, the more you'll understand it."

"So, are you ever going to tell us what this reverend person actually said?" Dad was arranging the avocado and red pepper slices on top of the lettuce in the salad bowl, his back to the two women.

Mom licked her lips and looked at Monica; I sat forward in my seat. "Reverend Irene looked at me for a few seconds and then she started to talk. She talked quickly and I couldn't get all of it—Monica took some notes for me. She said there was a tall woman . . ." Mom's tear ducts began to overflow, but she was smiling at the same time. I got the tissue box and set it on the table, but she didn't take one. "A tall woman who was always with me. That sounds like Bunny, doesn't it? She said there were vases standing all around her, which probably has something to do with my studio, my pots, and then she got off on some track I couldn't quite follow about sledding in the winter and a sign over a garage window. . . ."

Monica had fished a notebook out of her big satchel. "The sign said, 'Hot Dogs and Pickles.' And then she went on about breaking cups and saucers and being sorry about it. That didn't make sense to you at the time, but you may come to understand it more later on. That often happens."

Mom nodded. "And then Reverend Irene said the woman was holding a white rose in her hand. I didn't get that either, but then Monica told me later that a white rose is symbolic of a celebration of some sort. That's when I knew it really was Bunny." Her tears were flowing, but Mom still smiled, like a rainbow at the end of a storm. "She would remember that, and she would know that *I'd* remember."

I looked at Dad who was taking the pizza out of the oven. He seemed as confused as I was.

"It's not our anniversary," he said. "It's not your birthday. Am I forgetting something?"

"It was *their* anniversary," she said, her voice breaking. "Bunny and Dad. June thirtieth. *Today.*"

The dinner table fell silent after Dad said, "That is the most ridiculous thing I've ever heard." He sawed the pizza into eight sloppy pieces and threw two slices onto each of our plates, then filled his wine glass and slugged half of it down in one gulp. His ears got very pink at their tips.

Monica and Mom exchanged wise looks, and then ate their pizza without a word.

I was so confused I could hardly taste my dinner. Dad was angry, that much was obvious. But my father *never* got angry, at least not at me or Mom. He might be *disappointed* with me sometimes, if I wasn't "working up to my potential," as he called it. And I'd always thought his disappointment was worse than having him just yell at me, but I certainly didn't like this silent, red-faced *mad* that was brewing inside him now.

And I hated that it was directed at Mom. After the last few weeks he ought to be glad she was so happy, even if he didn't believe in Spiritualism. I'd almost rather he was angry at *me*. God, I couldn't remember my parents ever being really mad at each other. They had disagreements sometimes, but it never turned mean like with Roxanne's parents. Once, when I was younger, I got so scared when Rox's father started yelling at her mother that I ran home crying. I didn't know parents could dislike each other that much, even momentarily. Except now my dad was furious because Mom had gone to a church where they talked to dead people. Who would have thought *that* would drive him over the edge?

Monica left as soon as dinner was over, and I went upstairs, saying I had a book to read. I had a feeling they wanted to talk, so I perched at the top of the stairs and listened. At first the only sound was the clanking of silverware and dishes being rinsed and put into the dishwasher.

Finally Dad broke the silence. "A *white rose*?" he said.

"Some of these symbols are very well documented," Mom said. "Monica has a book about it. A white rose almost always means celebration."

"Christine," Dad said, sounding more sad now than

angry. "I know you miss Bunny terribly. I really do understand that, but going to these crackpots and buying into all this trash they're selling . . ."

"They aren't *selling* anything."

"A regular church would be bad enough, but *this*," he said. "Don't you see how foolish this is?"

"Jack, you weren't there. You don't know what it's like. The mediums . . . they really contact spirits. I could feel it."

"I know you want to believe this, Christine, but all that silly stuff this woman told you—"

"Reverend Irene, and she's not 'silly.'"

"Whoever she is. She just gives people a bunch of words that they can read their own ideas into. A *tall woman*? That could be a million different people. Garages and teacups and white roses—to somebody else the hot dog sign would probably mean something. If they toss out enough nouns, something is bound to sound familiar. Don't you see that?" At least Dad didn't sound so awfully angry now. If only he could just forget about it. It made Mom happy!

"I understand what you're saying, but, Jack . . . Bunny was there."

Dad sighed as though he were pulling the frustration up from the bottoms of his feet.

"Next time," Mom said, "I want you and Liz to come with me. So you can understand it. So you—"

"Absolutely not!" Dad's voice was so loud and harsh I jumped. Never had my father spoken to my mother like that. "You are *not* taking my daughter to that so-called church! I can't stop you if you want to go back yourself, but not with Liz. No! I absolutely *forbid* it!"

"Jack, she's my daughter too. You're not being fair."

"I don't give a damn about *fair!*" he yelled, and then something shattered against the kitchen wall and I jumped up from the stairs. "There!" he said. "There's your broken cup and saucer! I've fulfilled the prophecy! Does that make you happy?"

Shaking, I felt my way down the dark hallway to my room. I couldn't stand to hear any more. My father never spoke like that to *anyone*. That he could yell at *Mom,* who'd just started to smile again after weeks of crying, that he could forbid me to go with her even though she really wanted me to, made me suddenly hate him. I knew I probably wouldn't hate him forever, but I hated him now, for the pain that I felt spreading across my chest and that I knew Mom must be feeling too.

I *would* go to Singing Creek with my mother, no matter *what* he said.

Chapter Five

When I came downstairs the next morning, Dad was gone. There was a note on the table saying he'd be at his elementary school. Something about looking through a shipment of new textbooks—like that's something he'd do on a Sunday. The kitchen was all clean and Mom was sitting at the table drinking coffee.

"Want me to make you some eggs?" she asked, but she looked like she didn't really want to get up.

I shook my head. "I'll just have cereal." We were obviously going to pretend nothing had happened the night before.

Mom sighed. "I think I'll open the studio today. Do you want to help me? The weather's nice—might be some traffic."

That was good news. I couldn't believe how excited I

was to hang out in a dusty room helping my mother on such a pretty weekend day. I knew I'd never be able to take Bunny's place in Mom's studio, but I started thinking maybe someday we'd sit on high stools and drink coffee and she'd talk to me about her work. I'd know just what she meant and we'd laugh and it would be great. Someday.

After breakfast I put the open-studio sign out by the road while Mom dusted shelves and rearranged her finished pots. She didn't unwrap the pieces she'd been working on, though. And she didn't put on her overalls and wedge a new batch of clay. She didn't actually *work* in the studio—she just sat there on the old, clay-covered chair with the broken springs and looked around as though it was a place she'd never seen before. Still, I told myself it was a move in the right direction. Since she wasn't in a talking mood, I got a book to read while we waited for customers.

Around noon a couple came by with two very active young boys. Normally, kids racing around the studio made Mom nervous and she'd suggest to their parents that the children might rather play outside on the lawn while they shopped. But today she just sat in that crummy chair with an empty smile on her face. She didn't say a word when I managed to catch a vase the boys bumped into—before it fell to the floor and smashed. The parents were embarrassed though: They yelled at the boys, then left without buying anything.

Later in the afternoon a gay couple stopped in and spent

a long time looking at Mom's brightly glazed work, the stuff she showed in galleries. Sure enough, they picked out two large blue garden jars and, after putting them in the trunk of their car, came back in and bought a set of eight mugs, too. This was a very big sale—the pots were expensive—and normally Mom would be chatting up customers who spent that much money with her.

But she just sat there as I took their credit card, wrapped and bagged the mugs, and told them to come back again. When I looked over at her, I could see that energy was leaking out of her like air from a knifed tire. I wondered if the customers had even realized that the artist was sitting right there, spacing out before their eyes.

At three o'clock Mom announced she was going to take a nap. "Would you bring the sign in, Liz? I don't think we'll get anybody else today." I thought of arguing that, in fact, people often stopped here in the late afternoons on their way back from the lake or from a picnic on Goat Mountain. I could have offered to sit in the studio myself for a few more hours. But why bother? I was as tired as she was of pretending everything was normal.

I hadn't seen Nathan and Courtney all day, and I hoped Mrs. Crosby hadn't kicked them out already. But when I went out to get the sign, there they were, Courtney playing with a Barbie doll on the rickety porch, Nathan sitting on the front steps staring at his shoes.

If such intriguing strangers had moved in across the

street from Roxanne, she would already know all about them; by now they would either be fast friends or sworn enemies. Which is why, when Roxy called me last night, I didn't tell her about my new neighbors. I knew she'd come running over to meet them and I wanted to keep them to myself for a while. They were *my* neighbors. Besides, Roxanne is terrible at keeping secrets. What if Nathan told her about his mother and she let it slip to Courtney? I could imagine her doing that and then saying, "She was going to find out anyway, sooner or later." As if that made it okay.

"Hi!" Courtney said as I came down the lawn. "Can you play?"

Nathan turned to Courtney and said something I couldn't hear.

Courtney looked aggravated but shouted to me again. "I'm not allowed to cross the street. Can you come over here?"

I folded up the sign and laid it flat on the ground. I didn't really want to spend my time putting outfits on Barbie, but I liked Courtney, and I was curious about Nathan. Besides, I felt sorry for them; not only was their mother dying, but they were stuck with the meanest grandmother on earth.

"I guess so," I said.

"Yeah!" Courtney shouted, twirling in circles. I laughed. It had been a long time since anybody had been *that* excited about having me around.

As I crossed the street, Nathan turned back to studying his sneakers, obviously less thrilled by my presence than his sister was.

"Do you want to play Barbies?" Courtney said. "I have three of them. You can use whichever one you want!"

"God, Courtney, she's too old to play with dolls," Nathan grumbled. "*You're* practically too old."

But Courtney was deaf to her brother's criticisms. She sat down on the porch floor and patted an old rocking chair that was missing half its seat. "You can have the chair. And you can have hip-hop Barbie—she's the best one."

I perched on the edge of the chair, suddenly aware that I was in hostile territory, and took the naked doll Courtney handed me. I'd forgotten how unreal these things looked with their ridiculously long legs, pointy boobs, and high-heeled feet. "She's a pretty one," I lied. "Should I put some clothes on her?"

"You don't have to play with her," Nathan said without turning around.

"I don't mind," I said, taking the mismatched outfit Courtney handed me.

Courtney stuck her tongue out at her brother. "See? She doesn't mind playing Barbies. She *likes* Barbies."

"I used to have Barbies too," I said. "But Woody chewed most of them up when he was a puppy."

"Did you ever have a Sweetheart doll?" Courtney asked. "That's what I *really* want."

"Dream on," Nathan said sourly. "Those dolls are for rich kids."

"I never had one either," I told Courtney. "They're really expensive."

"Yeah, I know," she said, "but I can still *want* one."

"So, are you all unpacked?" I asked as I pulled a slippery gown over Hip-Hop's head.

"No, we had to go to the hospital last night," Courtney reported matter-of-factly. "Mommy got sick again, but now she's better. We stayed up really late and slept all morning. Mommy slept at the hospital."

I glanced at Nathan, who sat motionless.

"Oh," I said, my heart suddenly beating too quickly. "Well, I'm glad she got better." Now I wished that Nathan hadn't told me the truth. It made me feel like a big liar in front of Courtney. I guess it made him feel that way too.

"Gramma said she'll probably come back here tomorrow afternoon."

I smiled and held up my no-longer-naked doll. "How do you like this dress?"

Behind us Mrs. Crosby had sneaked up to the porch door in her house slippers. When she suddenly said "Courtney!" in that loud, nasty voice of hers, we all jumped half a foot.

"God, Gramma, you scared me!" Courtney said.

"Criminy, if you don't stop the swearing, I'm gonna hang ya from the apple tree by one leg!"

"I wasn't swearing."

"You don't even know you're doin' it! That mother of yours . . ." Mrs. Crosby stopped and calmed herself down a little. "I need you to come in here and help me in the kitchen. It's about time you learned to be useful. Peel some potatoes and wash the spinach."

"If I have to help, so does Nathan!" Courtney said.

"There'll be plenty yard work for him to do later. Kitchen is women's territory. Come on, now."

I was shocked. I guess I knew there were people who still believed things like that, that men couldn't cook or do housework, but I'd never actually heard anybody *say* it before.

"But it's not *fair*," Courtney whined. "I'm playing with Liz."

Mrs. Crosby stared at me as though she'd never seen me before. "Life ain't always fair," she said, though her voice was softer now. "You'll have time for play when your work's done."

"I'll help too," Nathan said, standing up, resigned to his fate.

"No, you won't. It's my kitchen and I won't have you messin' it up."

Nathan stared at her, his mouth open. "Why do you think I'd—"

"'Cause I know men. They got two left hands, two left feet, and half a brain. Courtney, come in here now and stop complainin'." She held the door open and Courtney stomped inside, a scowl on her face.

Once they'd disappeared, Nathan kicked at the shaky porch railing. "I can't believe that's what we got for a grandmother. She's a lunatic!"

I nodded. "I coulda told you that."

Nathan looked at me for the first time since I'd crossed the street. "Yeah? Wouldn't have helped me. I'm stuck here anyway." He flopped back down on the steps.

Cautiously I sat down a few steps above him. "I guess Courtney doesn't know yet?" I whispered.

"You got that right."

I didn't know what else to say, so I didn't say anything. Now that I'd sat down, it seemed awkward to get right up again and leave.

After a minute Nathan said, "Mom's scared to tell her."

"Because Courtney'll be so upset?"

He shrugged. "Yeah, that. But also, with Courtney not knowing, the rest of us have to act like we don't know either. Once Courtney knows . . . well, that's it, no more pretending."

The awfulness of Nathan and Courtney's life suddenly overwhelmed me. It had been bad enough to lose Bunny, but to lose a *parent*—even one who was currently acting weird—that I couldn't imagine.

"My grandmother died a few weeks ago," I said, and immediately wished I hadn't. It wasn't the same thing.

Bunny's child was a grown-up woman—even though she didn't always act like one—but Nathan's mother had two children who still needed her around.

"Yeah?" he said. "I wish it was *my* grandmother dying instead of my mother."

I was shocked at the hatred in his voice. "My grandmother wasn't like *yours*. She was really cool and she wasn't even that old. Everybody liked Bunny."

"Bunny?" Nathan said.

"That's what we called her. It's a nickname for Elizabeth."

"So, you're named after her," he said.

I nodded though he wasn't looking at me. "But I'm nothing like her."

"Nobody is like anybody else. That's why nobody gets along with anybody else."

Lord, he was gloomy. Not that I wouldn't have been too in his circumstances, but still, it wasn't exactly what I needed these days.

"Some people get along," I said. "My mother got along great with Bunny."

He turned around. "Really?"

"Yes, really."

"Can you think of another example?"

Yesterday I would have said 'my parents,' but that didn't seem to be true anymore. There must be *some* other people who could tolerate each other. "I got along with Bunny too. Everybody got along with Bunny."

Nathan sniffed. "Okay, other than St. Bunny. I'm talking about ordinary people."

"You're just thinking this way because of your mother. Which I can understand. I'd feel miserable too if—"

"You have no idea how you'd feel!" he said, jumping up and walking onto the lawn.

I was quiet for a minute, then ventured, "Well, I can imagine—"

"No, you can't!" he insisted, freezing me to the step with his stare.

I sighed. "Okay! Maybe I can't! But I know I'd feel crappy and I think you're just feeling depressed—"

"Don't tell me what I'm feeling, okay? *Do not tell me what I'm feeling!* I'm sick to death of everybody telling me *what I'm feeling!*" The stairs threatened to collapse as he stomped up them. He threw open the screen door and let it hit against the porch wall. And was gone.

I got up quickly, angry and embarrassed at being yelled at like that, and was across the street before Mrs. Crosby could start hollering about not letting the door bang. If that's the way Nathan intended to act, I wasn't going to waste my sympathy on him. I'd try to help Courtney, if I could, once she heard the bad news. But I didn't care what happened to Nathan. He was as obnoxious as his grandmother.

I picked up the open-studio sign and lugged it back inside. Dad still wasn't home. And then I found Mom, back in her bed, the curtains closed against the sunlight. Shit. Just when things were starting to get a little better.

I sat down carefully on the side of Mom's bed, so as not to rock the mattress too much. "You're not feeling good?" I said.

She hummed an answer without words. Bad sign.

"Did you know that Mrs. Crosby's daughter and grandchildren moved in with her yesterday?"

I said it just for something to say—an excuse to stay there and talk to her—and was surprised when it got a response. Mom turned over and stared at me. "Her daughter? *Lily?* She's *back*?"

"Do you know her?"

Mom pulled herself into a sitting position, stuffing a pillow behind her neck. "I went to school with Lily from the time we were little kids. We were friends, sort of. Although she was a strange one. I always liked her, but I never really knew what was going on in her head. Right after we graduated from high school, she ran away. At least that's what I heard. I never knew where she went or what happened to her."

"Well, she's back. With two kids, Nathan and Courtney."

"Amazing! I never thought I'd see Lily again. She didn't get along with her mother. Mrs. Crosby was just as bullheaded then as she is now. Have you seen Lily?"

I shook my head. "I just met her kids. I guess she's kind of . . . sick." I hated having to tell Mom more bad news. "She has leukemia. But they haven't told the little girl yet."

Her hand flew over her mouth. "Oh, no. That's terrible!"

"I know."

She sighed. "I'll have to go over to see her. Maybe there's something I can do to help."

I was glad to see Mom interested in something other than herself, so I kept talking. "The little girl is really sweet, but the older boy is a jerk just like Mrs. Crosby."

"I'm sure he's having a hard time, Liz. Don't judge him too harshly. Losing your mother . . ." She stopped talking and closed her eyes.

Oh, no—I didn't want to go *there*. I rattled on. "I'm not judging him. I tried to be nice to him and he acted like an idiot."

Mom sat forward and threw her legs over the edge of the bed. "I should make something to take over there. I wonder what I've got in the house. I could make a coffee cake, maybe, or a pie. But I don't want it to seem funereal either." She was talking to herself now, but at least she was out of bed.

I started to leave the room, satisfied that she'd gotten up.

"Lizzie," Mom said as I was going out the door. "I wanted to ask you . . . I think I'm going to Singing Creek again next Saturday. Daddy doesn't want you to go, but if you want to come with me, you can. I think it should be your decision."

"I do want to," I answered quickly. "I want to talk to Bunny."

Mom smiled, almost a real smile. "Me too. But maybe we shouldn't get our hopes up. I mean, I don't know what really happened yesterday. Daddy thinks I'm being a fool and maybe I am. But I liked being there. I liked the people, their hopefulness. Your father is so . . . I don't know . . . *hateful* about anything religious."

"How come?"

Mom sighed as she brushed at her hair, quickly pulling it back into a low ponytail. "You don't remember your Scattergood grandparents—they died when you were just a baby. Even now I'm not sure I know the whole story. Relationships between parents and children can be so complicated."

No kidding.

"Are you sure you want to hear this? I don't know how interesting it will be to you," she said.

"I want to hear it," I said. And I did, but I also just wanted to hear my mother speak in whole long sentences again, like a normal person.

She sighed. "Well, your dad grew up going to church every Sunday—an Episcopal church. His parents were very devout, supposedly, and held positions on the church council and just about every committee that formed, I guess. Dad's father was very strict with him and punished him for the smallest infraction of the household rules. If he forgot to wipe his boots before he came inside, for example, his father whipped him with a belt and told him it was the

Lord's will. Your dad was always supposed to be perfect for *God*. Still, I think Jack was more afraid of his father than he was of God."

Mom sat down on the edge of the bed to finish her story. "Then when your dad was about thirteen, it came out that his very pious father had been stealing money from the church for years. Apparently, he was the treasurer of various committees and he just deposited some of the church's money into his own account."

I plunked down on the bed next to her, stunned. Dad's father was a thief? "Why would he do that? If he was so religious?"

She shrugged. "Sometimes people think they're above the laws the rest of us live by. They're blind to their own imperfections. That's what your dad says, anyway. Apparently, Mr. Scattergood had a girlfriend living in another town, and he needed money that your grandmother didn't know about to pay for her apartment."

My mouth was hanging open. "I can't believe this."

"Neither could your dad. He was raised to believe his father was God's lawmaker here on earth. And then he finds *this* out."

"So what happened?"

"Well, after people found out about it, your grandfather promised to pay the money back, and since the church didn't want the scandal in the papers, they didn't press charges. But everybody knew about it anyway, and your grandmother left him. Your father was humiliated but, I think, more than that, he felt foolish. All those years he'd believed in his father's righteous God, and suffered punishments as though he deserved them. And then to find out that his father was a liar and a thief himself—well, it soured your dad on religion and everyone who practices it. He gets livid on the subject, as you've seen. He says religion makes fools of people, but it was his father who deceived him, not God."

"How come I never heard this before?" I asked.

"Because your dad doesn't like to talk about it. And don't tell him I told you either. Religion is the one subject he gets riled up about. Well, religion and his father."

"Did Dad's father ever punish him again after that?"

"I don't think he dared try. Your father wouldn't have anything to do with him. He never went back to the church and he didn't even speak to his father for years."

"Wow. So that's why Dad won't go to church."

Mom nodded. "The whole incident left a bitter taste in his mouth. He says you don't need a church and a minister lecturing you in order to be a good person, and I think that's true, but maybe sometimes you need it for other reasons."

"Just because his father was dishonest doesn't mean everyone who goes to church is no good."

"I've said that to him, but he doesn't want to hear it."

Suddenly I realized I was having a real conversation with

my mother about important things. And we were agreeing about them too—just like she and Bunny had! "I want to go with you to Singing Creek, Mom, even if Dad doesn't want me to," I said.

She put her hands on my shoulders. "I'm glad, Liz. But let's not mention it to Dad right away, okay? He'll just stew about it from now until Saturday."

"Okay," I agreed. I knew Dad would be upset with my decision, and now I even knew why. But Mom was inviting me to join her, and I had to go. Mom and I had a secret. And it was the first time she'd touched me in weeks.

Chapter Six

I spent as much time that week as I could practicing for my recital on Friday. I didn't have a real summer job because I wouldn't be sixteen until the fall, so I did the same thing I'd done last year: babysitting. My schedule left plenty of time for piano-playing; I worked every day from eleven to five watching Emma and Jake, five-year-old twins, while their mother went shopping or went swimming or played tennis.

The Romanows had a summer house on Monticook Lake, which was about half a mile from our house. They called it a cottage, but it was bigger than most people's regular homes. Mrs. Romanow and the twins spent the whole summer here and Mr. Romanow came out from Boston on the weekends. I got the job last year when Mrs. Romanow came into Mom's studio to order an entire set of dishes for their summer house, and I kept the twins entertained on the lawn while the adults talked. Mrs. Romanow paid me well and gave me tips besides, and Jake and Emma were easy to deal with, so all in all it was a pretty cushy job.

Roxanne asked me how much I was making, and when I told her, she was amazed. "That's more than I make working at the garden center!"

"Per hour, maybe, but you work more hours."

She scowled. "Yeah, and I also lug around forty-pound bags of mulch and potting soil. My back is broken by the time I finish a weekend shift. All you have to do is play Candy Land and hand out Popsicles."

That wasn't *all* I did, but I let it go. "Think how much money you'll have by the end of the summer," I reminded her.

"Big deal," she said. "Dad says I have to put it all in the bank and save it for college."

I hated having these arguments about whose life was tougher. Nobody could really win them, anyway, since neither of our lives were all that bad.

On Monday, Lily came home from the hospital. I saw her first, crawling carefully out of the backseat of Mrs. Crosby's ancient car. I called to Mom, and she watched too as Nathan walked his frail mother up the path to the front door while Courtney ran ahead to open it and Crabby fussed around her car, making sure no one had gotten a speck of dirt on it, I guess.

"My God, I can't believe that's Lily," Mom said, shaking her head. "She looks so *small.*"

"Was she bigger when you knew her?"

"Much. She wasn't heavy, but she was robust, healthy, athletic. She was the kind of girl who would sit down at the table and take seconds on everything that came around twice. And then go outside and play baseball with the boys for hours. She rode horses too. During high school she worked at the Kean Stables in Chesterton."

It made me shiver to think of the sick woman who was inching her way up the porch steps as young and healthy, riding horses, playing baseball. Life could change so quickly.

"It must gall her to come back here and ask her mother for help," Mom said. "After all these years."

"And Mrs. Crosby's not making it easy either," I said. "At least, she's not very nice to her grandchildren."

Mom sighed. "What is wrong with that woman, anyway? I'm going over there right now with my pie, before Lily falls asleep. Do you want to come with me?"

Did I want to meet a woman my mother's age who was dying? Did I want to face Nathan, who'd yelled at me the last time I was over there? Did I want to talk to Courtney, who might know the truth by now? No, no, and no. It was all too awful. I told Mom I needed to practice some more.

She shook her head as though my practicing were a bad habit. "I swear, Lizzie, you're going to wear your fingers down to the bone."

. . .

The Romanows had a piano in their "cottage," so one afternoon I entertained the twins by playing a few simple songs for them to sing along with. Then Emma decided she wanted to learn to play the piano too, and Jake wanted to do everything Emma did, so before I knew it, I was teaching them both how to play scales and pick out "Twinkle, Twinkle, Little Star." When their mother got home, they showed her their new skills.

"That's wonderful! Liz, I can't believe you taught them all this in one afternoon," Mrs. Romanow said.

"It was fun," I told her. "We were just playing around."

"It hadn't occurred to me to start them with piano lessons this early, but I'd love it if you'd teach them more when you're here."

I hesitated. "Well, if they want to. Sometimes if you *have* to do something, it isn't as much fun."

Mrs. Romanow nodded. "You are wise beyond your years, Liz. Tell you what, on the days they want a lesson, I'll give you an extra twenty dollars. You just let me know, okay?"

"Really?"

"Believe me, if I took them to a *real* teacher, I'd pay much more than that."

I guess I was too young to be a real anything. Still, I wasn't going to refuse a chance to make some extra money, so Emma and Jake became my first piano students.

When I got home, I figured out how much money I could make during the summer, even if I only gave the twins lessons twice a week. It was more money than I'd ever had before, and I felt like I ought to figure out something really special to do with it. Unlike Roxanne's parents, mine wouldn't make me put it away for college. Bunny had put money in a trust for me so my college would be paid for—she'd told me that herself several years ago.

What did I really want? I wanted to go somewhere. Take a trip. See something I hadn't seen before. We never took vacations because Mom kept the studio open in the summers—that's when she made her money—and the rest of the year Dad and I were in school. Oh, we went into Boston sometimes during school vacation week, or drove up into Vermont for a few days, and that was fun.

But last summer Bunny had taken me to New York City for a week. She went to New York and Chicago and San Francisco a lot to visit galleries and museums and go to concerts, and she'd wanted to take me along before, but Mom always said I wasn't old enough to appreciate it and would just be an annoyance. Which always pissed me off. I would have appreciated *anything* Bunny showed me. Anyway, last year Bunny insisted I go with her, and Mom finally gave in. To tell you the truth, I think she was a little jealous that she couldn't go too.

We had the best time. We went to the big museums like

MoMA and the Metropolitan, and to a bunch of little galleries too. We heard Yo-Yo Ma and saw *Wicked* on Broadway and *Cat on a Hot Tin Roof* in a tiny theater in SoHo. We ate Indian food and Korean food and Turkish food and the best cheesecake I'd ever had. We stayed in a huge hotel near Rockefeller Center that had murals in the lobby and televisions in the bathrooms. We walked down Canal Street and through Times Square, Greenwich Village, and Central Park. We went to a used bookstore that was bigger than my elementary school. And we took taxis everywhere.

I felt a little bit like a hick from the country. Everybody in New York seemed all dressed up and in a hurry—busy and important—while we were sauntering along in our T-shirts and Tevas. Because of all the tall buildings, I kept feeling like I was never really outside, which made me a little nervous. I couldn't imagine living in a place like that, but visiting it was great. There was so much to see and do, you could never be bored. You were the opposite of bored. It was almost too much, but not quite.

Bunny enjoyed herself too. When we were driving back home, she said, "We should have done this years ago. I don't know why I let your mother talk me out of it. I should have just kidnapped you!"

"You should have," I said. "Mom wouldn't even have noticed I was gone."

Bunny got a worried look on her face. "You don't really believe that," she said.

I did believe it, but I didn't want to upset Bunny, so I just smiled at her as if I'd been joking.

Bunny was an expert driver; she whizzed around trucks and busses until before I knew it we were out of the city. We were somewhere around Hartford, Connecticut, I think, when she reached over and squeezed my knee.

"You're my favorite traveling companion, Lizzie," she said. "We appreciate the same things. From now on you're coming with me whenever possible."

Of course, we didn't know it would never be possible again. Just knowing that I'd never take another trip with Bunny made me tear up a little. Thank God Mom let me go last year. Bunny had shown me what to look at and how to really *see* what I was looking at—things I would have been too overwhelmed to notice otherwise. What if I'd never had the chance to see New York through Bunny's eyes?

So, yes, I wanted to travel, to see other amazing cities and countries. Bunny had shown me how to do it. And if I could save up the money, maybe I'd get to Chicago and San Francisco by myself.

Having Lily across the street had at least gotten Mom out of bed. She still wasn't working in her studio, but at least she changed out of her pajamas in the mornings. She kept trying to get me to go over to Mrs. Crosby's house with her when she visited Lily, but I had the excuse of the recital. What excuse would I use next week?

Dad was acting normal again and fixing dinner for us at night while Mom told stories she and Lily had prodded each other into remembering.

"Lily had some Bunny stories I'd totally forgotten," Mom said. "She reminded me of a party we'd gone to when we were just little kids. We were supposed to play Pin-the-Tail-on-the-Donkey, but Lily didn't want to be blindfolded—the dark scared her—and some overbearing parent was trying to talk her into doing it anyway. But Bunny came to her rescue and told the woman, 'For God's sake, let that child keep her eyes open!' Doesn't that sound just like Bunny?"

I was glad that Mom was able to talk about Bunny now without getting so upset. She was remembering the good times.

"I guess Lily was crazy about Bunny," Mom continued. "She also remembered that for my birthday one year—I must have been nine or ten—Bunny bought straw hats for all the girls to decorate. We were out in the barn at our house on Water Street so we could make a big mess. She had spray paint, plastic flowers, felt, beads, buttons, ribbons—all kinds of stuff for us to stick on our hats. Of course, I was used to making things since that was Bunny's favorite activity, but for Lily this apparently opened a whole new window onto the world.

"She said it had never occurred to her before that people actually *made* things like hats. Isn't that funny? She said she remembers designing hers very carefully, spraying the whole hat red and then using as many of the plastic flowers as possible. Of course, Mrs. Crosby stood in the doorway while Lily was telling me this, and she had to put in her two cents' worth. She shook her head in disgust and said, 'What a hideous creation that was.' I imagine that's what she said at the time, too.

"But apparently Lily loved that hat and wore it around the house for *years*. Making it had been very important to her, she said. She'd never made anything before. After she moved away, she started making jewelry—and she credits Bunny with getting her interested in the arts."

"Bunny affected more people than she knew," Dad said quietly.

Mom nodded.

"What happened to the hat?" I asked quickly, hoping Mom wouldn't start to dwell on Bunny's death again.

"Lily didn't say, but I'd be very surprised if her mother didn't manage to throw it out when Lily wasn't looking."

"That's probably what'll happen to Courtney's Barbie dolls too," I said. "You can't trust Mrs. Crabby."

Dad paused in his stir-frying. "You two! Mrs. Crosby is an old woman who hasn't had an easy life. You could be a bit more charitable."

"Jack, I've known the woman for years. She's always been bad-tempered and disagreeable. Look, she drove her own daughter out of the house!"

"We don't know all the circumstances surrounding that," Dad said. "You could give her the benefit of the doubt."

Mom sighed. "You give everyone the benefit of the doubt. They don't always deserve it."

"Well, sometimes they do. Didn't you tell me her husband left her when Lily was very young? That was unusual in those days."

"Who could live with *her*?" I put in, happy to be able to take Mom's side. "The poor guy probably ran for his life."

Dad looked unhappy. "It's disrespectful for you to say such mean things about an elderly woman, Liz."

My mouth dropped open. "Mom's saying it too!"

"Well, your mother is an adult. I can't tell her what to do, but I can tell you." He spooned the stir-fry over rice on the plates. I loved Dad's chicken stir-fry, but there was a funny taste in my mouth from being scolded, which made that night's dinner taste like cardboard cooked in glue.

Especially since Mom didn't even come to my rescue. She passed me a plate without comment, took her own, and began to pick through the pea pods and chicken pieces with her chopsticks. She was a million miles away already, probably remembering some wonderful time she'd had with Bunny. Some time that didn't include me.

Chapter Seven

I probably should have worked at the Romanows' on Friday to keep my mind off the recital, but instead I decided to practice all afternoon. My piano teacher, Mr. Bellerose, had told us to try to relax the day of the performance, but I knew that was out of the question for me. I was so nervous I couldn't even get through my Scott Joplin pieces without a million mistakes, much less the Mozart sonata or the Debussy. Which made me more nervous than ever. I was beginning to think I wouldn't be able to do it, wouldn't even be able to walk out onto the stage at the Grange Hall without collapsing into a sweaty puddle. I reminded myself that I felt this way every year and somehow I always got through it.

Dad made chicken soup for dinner because he said it was easy to digest. Trust Dad to realize I'd need intravenous comfort. I sipped it cautiously and munched a lot of saltine crackers. I could tell Dad was trying to think of things to talk about other than the concert, but I wasn't very responsive. When there's an elephant in the room, you can't pretend it isn't there and just discuss the ants.

I was glad to see that even though she'd slept until noon, Mom had dressed nicely for the recital. I had on my concert outfit: a long black skirt and a white silk blouse, which was really a little too tight in the chest. I must have gotten bigger since last year, which was the last time I'd worn the blouse. Neither Mom nor I had thought to check if my concert clothes still fit. Too late to do anything about it now.

As we walked outside, Mom said, "Bunny always loved going to your recitals."

I'd been thinking the same thing but hadn't said it for fear it would set Mom off. I looked anxiously at her face. She was perched on the edge of tears.

Dad was still inside searching for the car keys so I said, "Tomorrow! We're going to talk to Bunny tomorrow, remember? At Singing Creek."

Her forehead smoothed out again. "Yes, we are. Tomorrow. I can hardly wait." She gave me a tiny smile. Thank God, one crisis averted.

When we got to the Grange, the parking lot was three-quarters full. For a minute I panicked, but then I remembered that lots of old people in Tobias come to stuff like this. It was nice: They applauded loudly and called you "dear" afterward. Mom said they'd go to anything that was held in Tobias because they didn't like to drive the twenty minutes into Waverly. They called Waverly "the city," even though it had a population of only about forty thousand people. Mom could never understand why all older people weren't as fearless as Bunny was.

Mom and Dad took seats about halfway back in the auditorium, where the acoustics were the best. Roxanne and Paul were sitting right in the front row. God, I couldn't believe she'd made him come. He'd be asleep before Becky Murray got offstage. At least they hadn't brought Dan or one of Paul's other friends along.

Mr. Bellerose was standing backstage with Becky and Carlin, the two seventh graders who were playing before me. "Ah, good, you're here," he said. "I was beginning to worry."

"Dad couldn't find the car keys," I said.

Mr. Bellerose's eyes seemed to be having difficulty remaining on my face—they kept flickering farther south. I crossed my arms in front of the tight blouse. Mr. Bellerose was about one hundred and fifty years old, so I was sort of creeped out that he'd be looking at my boobs.

"Okay," he said, turning away. "Carlin and Liz, why don't you sit over there and breathe deeply. Becky, you wait here. We'll get started in just a minute."

Carlin, who always wore white dresses and white flats to her recitals—which seems to me to be the definition of a person who never expects to make a mistake—perched on the edge of her chair. "Your blouse is gaping," she said, pointing to the spot where the tiny bow on the front of my bra could be seen.

"I know," I said, sitting up straight and trying to make my breasts smaller. "I didn't realize it until it was too late. Do you think the audience will notice?"

She shook her head. "Nah. Well, maybe the first few rows."

Great.

Becky played fifteen nerve-wracking minutes and Carlin twenty flawless ones. Then it was my turn. I had to fill almost forty minutes. Mr. Bellerose gave a gushy introduction about what a hardworking, gifted pupil I was. Of course, I was the only one who'd taken lessons for eight years. It would be really embarrassing if I wasn't halfway decent after that long.

The andante from Mozart's Sonata in C Major was my first piece. It was my idea to do it first, because I usually do it pretty cleanly, and it seems to calm me down. Before I sat on the piano bench, I glanced out at the audience, toward the center where I knew Mom and Dad were. When I saw who was seated next to them, I'm sure my face registered the shock I felt. There sat Lily, Nathan, and Courtney Arnold, staring up at me.

Had Mom invited them to come? And if so, why hadn't she mentioned it to me? Now, on top of not making a fool of myself in front of my parents, my best friend, her boyfriend, and fifty old geezers, I had to worry about them too.

I sat down, closed my eyes, and told myself it didn't matter who was in the audience. Mr. Bellerose always reminded us to sit quietly at the piano for a moment before starting to play, to calm ourselves down, but it would have taken a Zen master to calm me down. Still, once I started the andante, it went pretty smoothly—some timing goofs, but that was all. And by the end of it the music itself had calmed me, which was one of the things I loved about playing the piano.

Next came the Debussy piece, "Children's Corner." It lasted fifteen minutes or so and some of it was very fast. It was the hardest piece I'd ever played and I'd never really done it perfectly. Mr. Bellerose had assured me this audience wouldn't notice and I should just play it in "a lively manner." But I couldn't relax into it the way I had the Mozart. I kept wondering whether Roxy and Paul could see the gap in my blouse. If my mom was thinking about me or about Bunny. Whether Lily was enjoying herself. If Nathan and Courtney were bored out of their minds. I made mistakes at the places I usually made mistakes, and then, because I was shaken up, I made more besides. Amazingly, when I was finished, the audience clapped a long time, and somebody, probably Roxanne, hooted.

I had purposely left the Scott Joplin ragtime pieces for last. They were fast and fun, both to play and to listen to. I could usually whiz through them without much trouble, and anyone who'd been bored by the classical music would leave thinking they'd had a good time anyway.

With the Debussy behind me and the concert almost over, I was pretty relaxed. I loved doing the ragtime music—some of the pieces got really wild and I even bounced up and down on the bench a little bit, which Mr. Bellerose encouraged, calling it "showmanship."

And then, of course, it happened. Near the end of the second of my three Joplin numbers, I spread my arms to bang out the notes at either end of the piano—I was really into it—when suddenly the two buttons that were barely holding my blouse closed gave up the struggle, simultaneously leaping into the air like popcorn kernels and exposing my bra to a lot more than the first few rows.

This was not my first recital. I know you never just stop in the middle of a piece, no matter *what* happens. I hesitated for half a second, then sped through the rest of the number faster than humanly possible, stood up, bowed (holding my shirt closed with one hand), and walked off the stage. The hell with the third piece. Applause began slowly but built steadily. Some idiot was even stamping her feet like she was at a rock concert—as though I'd show my face onstage for an encore after that.

Mr. Bellerose and the two younger girls met me as I came racing offstage. Mr. Bellerose looked like a basset hound with his watery old eyes. "I was afraid . . . ," he mumbled, patting my shoulder awkwardly. Becky and Carlin kept leaping around me, saying, "Oh, my *God*! Oh, my *God*!" until I thought I might have to smother them. I held the two sides of my silk blouse, the betrayer, in a death grip.

Becky's mother was the first audience member to make it back to us, and she immediately put her black scarf around my shoulders, whispering to me, "You were wonderful. Wear this home—I'll get it another time." I *loved* her for that, but I couldn't even say thank you because my voice had apparently disappeared.

Roxanne came back with Dad. "Good Lord, what the hell happened?" she yelled at me.

"I think you saw what happened," I said, the voice making an abrupt return.

"But, I mean, how come you wore such a tight shirt? You're a lot bigger than you were last year, you know."

I was not going to start bawling in front of all these people. "Roxanne, I just didn't think about it . . . and then it was too late."

"Didn't your *mother* say anything? I'm surprised she let you go out like—"

Dad stepped in front of Roxanne and put an arm around my shoulders. "I'm sorry, sweetheart. I wish I'd realized you needed a new blouse. It didn't take away from your playing, though. The audience loved your performance."

Yeah, yeah, what do you expect your father to say?

"My dad would never have noticed either, but *Mom*

would have," Roxy repeated, just in case I hadn't understood her the first time. There were tears ready to spill down my face, but I fought them back. I was not going to embarrass myself even more by bawling like an infant.

"But the concert was fantastic, Lizzie," Dad said, working hard to pretend this was not the most mortifying moment of my life so far. "Really fantastic. You're getting better and better."

Now that I was no longer half-naked, Mr. Bellerose came up to me again too. "Yes, my dear, you've made great strides this year. Your work is lovely."

"Thank you." Maybe Mr. B could overlook it, but I was quite certain the aspect of the concert most people would remember was the floor show.

"You *were* really good, Liz," Roxanne said finally. "Even Paul liked it. Especially the grand finale." She laughed. I didn't.

Mom's old friends Eva and Rosemarie were waiting for me as I walked out the front door. Eva gave me a hug and Rosemarie kissed my cheek.

"You were great, sweetie," Eva said.

Rosemarie gazed at me sadly. "We've missed you!"

"Thanks," I said. "I haven't seen you guys in ages."

They both glanced up at Dad, then smiled at me. "Maybe we'll come by one of these days. It's just, you know, your mom has been so . . . busy," Eva said.

'Busy' was not the right word for what Mom was, but

none of us wanted to search for a more accurate one. Eva and Rosemarie hurried off to their cars.

"Where's Mom?" I asked Dad.

He gestured toward the parking lot. "She's waiting with Lily and her kids. Lily was hoping to meet you."

Oh, God, what else? Couldn't this day just be *over*? Now I had to go act normal in front of those people I'd been avoiding all week. With a black shawl draped over my exploded blouse and too-big boobs. Well, at least I'd given that gloomy Nathan something to laugh about.

Paul was waiting outside too, standing there talking to Nathan, of all things. I guess it wasn't that strange since they were the only teenage boys in the place, but still. Of course, Roxanne headed right over there too.

Nathan's mother took my hand as soon as we got near them. "Hi, Liz. I'm Lily," she said. "I enjoyed your playing so much! I could tell a lot of work went into this concert."

She was thin, with just a fuzz of dark hair covering her scalp, but her eyes were sparkly, like Courtney's, and she didn't seem to me like a person who was dying. I mean, she didn't seem unhappy or upset or anything. She seemed like anybody else, which I guess was good.

"Oh, she practices around the clock," Mom said. "I wish I could get her to do something else once in a while." She smiled and pecked in the direction of my cheek. "You were good tonight, Lizzie. Despite playing in your underwear."

Was that supposed to be a joke? Ha-freaking-ha.

Courtney came running up from behind me and almost knocked me off my feet. "You played really good!" she said. "Oh, and don't worry. When your blouse came open, I put my hand over Nathan's eyes so he wouldn't look."

I glanced at Nathan to see if he'd heard her. He was looking back at me, with blush circles on his cheeks that almost matched my own. God, I was never going to be able to speak to him again.

A couple of brave old ladies came up to me then and congratulated me, called me "dear," and refrained from mentioning my disrobing. They didn't stick around long, though.

"Liz!" Roxanne said, running up to me. "Here's the plan. Nathan will take his mother and sister home—you go change your blouse—and then the two of you can meet us at O'Henry's. You must be starving, aren't you?"

I stared at her. In under five minutes she'd become Nathan's new buddy and had conjured up a future in which Nathan and I sat in a car together, alone, then spent the evening hanging out with her and Paul, impersonating a couple. And this was to occur on the same evening I had exposed myself to both boys in question (not to mention a large auditorium full of senior citizens). No, I didn't think so.

"What a good idea!" Lily said. "I've been hoping Nathan would meet some kids his age here and get away from us old ladies for a while."

Christ. Nathan didn't look pleased about it either, but

Roxanne was kissing up to Lily now too, and Mom was beaming. My fate was obviously sealed.

"Can I go too? I'm not an old lady!" Courtney said. "I want to get a dessert. Gramma never has dessert."

I was about to chime in that it was fine with me if Courtney came along, but Lily intervened before I could say anything. "You know what? Tomorrow we'll get some ice cream to keep at Grandma's house, okay? And some cookies, too."

I could tell Courtney was prepared to howl about the injustice of it all, but Lily quickly said good-bye to everyone and hustled her into their car. Nathan got into the driver's seat, silently, without even another glance in my direction.

Roxanne and Paul took off too, Roxy yelling, "See you in a little while!"

How had this happened? I couldn't sit in a booth at O'Henry's with Nathan and Paul. I was humiliated! I should be hiding under a big rock and eating worms tonight! Instead, I crawled numbly into the backseat of our car and wrapped the black shawl around myself so that it covered most of my miserable face.

"I'm glad you're getting to know Nathan," Mom said. "He's quiet, but he seems very sweet. He helps his mother so much and she adores him. She adores both those kids, you can tell."

Yes, I could tell. Parental love was pretty easy to spot. Anger was smoldering under the shawl, in my shaky chin, in my stinging eyes, and in my ruptured heart. I tried to hold it in, but it burst out along with the tears. "Didn't you know I'd need a new blouse? I've worn this one for three years already! How could you let me go out like that? This was my recital! Didn't you even look at me?"

Mom turned around in her seat, shocked. "Liz, for goodness' sake! You're not a baby—I don't dress you anymore. How is this *my* fault?" She turned to the front again. "You want to be treated like an adult, but you don't want the responsibility."

Of course she was right about the blouse. I should have tried it on sooner, but I was only worrying about my playing, not my outfit. Besides, Mom was acting as if the whole thing was funny instead of hideously embarrassing. Why couldn't she ever understand how I felt?

"Don't you get it?" I said, sobbing. "This was my recital! It was important!"

"Liz," Mom said, in her most patronizing voice, "it's not as if the *New York Times* was covering it. We'll get you a new blouse for next year."

"I'm not doing a recital next year!" I yelled.

She sighed and probably rolled her eyes at my stubborn childishness.

I could see Dad looking sympathetically into the rearview mirror. "Poor Lizzie. It's been a hard day for you. Tomorrow will be better."

Right, I thought. *Don't make promises you can't keep.*

Chapter Eight

Whether tomorrow would be better or not, I still had to get through the rest of tonight. I changed into jeans and a T-shirt and sat by the front window, wondering if Nathan would emerge from the house across the street or not. I was sure that, like me, he'd rather go to bed and forget the whole day ever happened.

Amazingly enough, the front door of Mrs. Crosby's dump opened and Nathan stepped out. He stood on the front porch looking over at our house as if he didn't know what he was supposed to do, or maybe trying to decide if he really *had* to take me with him to O'Henry's. After a minute he came down the porch steps and headed across the street.

I certainly didn't intend to have Mom and Dad involved in this any more than they already were, so I called upstairs, "I'm going. I'll be back in an hour or so."

"Have fun, honey!" Dad called down the stairs.

"Don't be shy," Mom said. "Nathan's probably more nervous than you are."

"Yeah," Dad agreed. "Boys are terminally terrified of females."

"It's no big deal—we're not trading saliva," I said, then ran out the door before they could send down any more dumb advice. God, it wasn't the seventies anymore. They didn't have a clue about teenage life, which was probably because so far I hadn't really had one that they could observe.

"Hey," Nathan said as I walked down the lawn to meet him.

"Hey," I answered.

"So, I have no idea where this O'Henry's place is," he said. His fists were stuffed into his pockets and his expression looked like he was headed to an execution rather than a restaurant.

"It's not far," I said. "Just off Route 10 on the way to Waverly."

"It's, like, a hangout, or what?"

I shrugged. "Sort of. Lots of kids go there. They have good fries and ice cream."

He nodded. "I'm not too big on hanging out, I guess."

Okay, you don't have to hit me with a hammer, I can take a hint. "We don't have to go. I'll tell Roxanne I was too tired. Which is true, anyway."

"You don't want to go?" He looked confused.

"Well, I mean, I'll *go,* but it's no biggie to me if you don't want to."

He sighed. "My mother wants me to. She thinks . . . I don't know . . . that being with other teenagers will make me normal again."

"Well, I guarantee hanging out with me won't make you normal," I said, going for a laugh. But he looked so sad, I felt sorry for him again, even though I'd told myself I wouldn't let that happen. "Look, let's just go to O'Henry's for a little while. We don't have to stay long."

He nodded, and we walked over to Mrs. Crosby's car. That thing was about as old as she was, but it started right up. "I'm surprised Crabby lets you use her car." As soon as I said it my hand flew up and covered my mouth. "Whoops."

"Crabby? That's what you call her? That's about right." He smirked. "She hates letting us use it, but I guess she feels sort of guilty about my mother. Which she should."

"Because she was so rotten to her when she was a teenager?"

He nodded and jerked the car into gear. "That, and other stuff."

"Why didn't you bring your own car?" I asked.

"We don't have one. We did, but we had to sell it a few months ago to pay Mom's medical bills. The chemo and stuff. Lot of good that did."

"Wouldn't her insurance pay for it?"

He shook his head. "She's self-employed—can't afford

health insurance. We had to sell just about everything we owned, which is why we ended up living with the Wicked Witch here in East Nowhere."

I sat back in the seat as if he'd hit me. I was shocked that they had no car and no health insurance—things I took for granted—and it was certainly awful to have to sell your stuff and move in with a mean old lady, but, for God's sake, what was so bad about living in Tobias? It wasn't *Nowhere*. It was a beautiful valley with lakes and farms and tree-lined roads. People came here on vacation. As much as I wanted to travel, I could never imagine any other place being my home.

"You don't like Tobias?" I asked.

"Why should I? There's nothing here but farms and hills."

"I like the farms and hills. And there are lakes, too, and great hiking trails—"

"On Cape Cod we're surrounded by water, the ocean on one side, the bay on the other. And we have these huge sand dunes, which are much better than regular hills—they shift and change from day to day. The whole landscape there is wild and gorgeous. This place just can't compare."

"So, I guess that's where you're from? Cape Cod?"

"That's my home," he said, "and it always will be."

Cape Cod. Whoop-de-freaking-do. I wasn't going to try to sell him on the Valley. If he couldn't see what was so great about it, it was his loss. This was *my* home, and the hell with him if he didn't like it.

We drove all the way to O'Henry's in silence except

when I had to give him directions. I might feel sorry for Nathan, but I didn't have to like him. He didn't seem to notice my aggravation, or maybe he just didn't care.

Roxanne and Paul were already squeezed together in a booth when we walked into O'Henry's. Rox waved and hollered, "Finally! I was starting to think you two ditched us to go off on your own."

I glared at her. Why does Roxanne just blurt out the first thing that comes into her mind? As if Nathan and I would have been together under any other circumstances except this arrangement she'd cooked up.

We slid into the other side of the booth, me pressed into the corner, Nathan on the outer edge of the seat. No mistaking us for a couple.

Roxanne and Paul were sharing a plate of onion rings and slurping on chocolate shakes. When the waitress came back around, I ordered fries and a vanilla shake. Nathan just asked for a Coke. I assumed he didn't want to stay long enough to eat an entire order of anything. No problem, I could get a ride back with Roxy and Paul if I had to, rather than endure another fifteen silent minutes in the Crabmobile.

"So, Nathan, you just moved here, right?" Roxanne began her interrogation. "And Mrs. Crosby is your grandmother? Paul just told me that—I could hardly believe it. Where did you move here from?"

Nathan fiddled with his napkin as he answered her. "We lived on Cape Cod, in Wellfleet. That's where I was born."

Oh, goody. More of the I-Heart-Cape-Cod travelogue.

"Really?" Roxy gushed. "I *love* Cape Cod! My family went to Brewster for two weeks one summer. We could walk to the beach from the house we rented. It was so cool. Could you walk to the beach from your house?"

Nathan nodded. "We were a few blocks from one of the bay beaches. I used to go clamming there with my friends. We sold them to the local market and still had enough for dinner anytime we wanted."

"Oh, that sounds like so much fun, doesn't it, Liz?" Roxy said, trying, I could tell, to pull me into the conversation. Unfortunately, I was in the middle of a flashback to the moment earlier in the evening when Scott Joplin had exposed more than my musical genius to half of Tobias.

"Yeah," was my brilliant response.

"I've been to Hyannis," Paul said. "We took a ferryboat to Nantucket from there. I'd love to live on the ocean like that."

"It was a great place. I really miss it," Nathan said with a forlorn grimace, as if he'd lost it forever. Then he turned to me. "Have you ever been to the Cape?"

I shook my head and sat up straighter in the booth. "We don't travel much in the summer. That's when my mother has her studio open."

"You live in Massachusetts and you've never been to Cape Cod? That's a crime! It's the most beautiful place in the state."

"I don't know about that," I said. "I think it's pretty nice right here." I wasn't going to let him get away with bashing the Valley again. He'd only been here a week. He hadn't even seen anything but Mrs. Crosby's backyard.

"Liz's mother is a potter," Roxy said, grinning at me. "She makes these beautiful platters and jars."

"Yeah, my mom told me. Apparently our mothers knew each other when they were kids."

"They did?" Roxanne cocked her head at me. "Geez, Liz, you never tell me anything. Were you hiding this guy or something? Keeping him all to yourself?"

"*Hiding* him? How could I . . . He just moved in a couple of . . . You are so insane, Roxanne." I was flustered by her silly questions and mad at myself for not being able to joke and banter as easily as she could. I felt like a total idiot.

"So, what does your mother do?" Rox continued questioning Nathan as if I hadn't said a word.

Nathan took a deep breath, then said, "She waits tables in the summer, and in the winter she makes jewelry to sell in the local shops. That's what she loves doing—making jewelry."

How did Roxanne get so good at talking to people? Why couldn't I do that?

Roxanne's eyes grew wide at the mention of jewelry. "Oh, wow, like necklaces and stuff? Earrings? Does she have any of it with her? Could I see it sometime?"

I wanted to slap a big hunk of duct tape over Roxanne's mouth.

Nathan shifted uncomfortably in the booth. "She has some. I'm sure she'd be happy to show it to you," he said, then focused on his drink. Obviously, he didn't want to talk about his mother.

Roxanne reached across the table and smacked my hand. "We'll have to go over and look at it!" she squealed.

To get her off the topic I thrust my dish of fries in front of her. "Have some," I said. "I can't eat all of these."

"Maybe Nathan wants some," she said, giving me a meaningful look as she took a handful herself.

"So, are you sticking around for a while?" Paul asked Nathan. "I belong to a summer basketball league. We could use a few more guys."

Nathan gave him half a smile. "Thanks, but I don't know how long we'll be here. It . . . depends."

"Depends on what?" Roxanne asked. "How come you came here in the first place? Just to see your grandmother? Isn't it awfully crowded staying in that little place?" Was there no way to shut her up?

I stole a glance at Nathan and saw his face turning pale. "We . . . uh . . . well, my mother . . . um . . ."

Obviously, he didn't want to announce his family problems to nosy Roxanne. I had to think of something to sidetrack her so she'd forget about her questions. The first thing that came to my mind worked better than I'd hoped.

"Oh, Roxanne," I said excitedly, "I almost forgot to tell you. Guess where my mom and I are going tomorrow?"

My eager tone got her attention. "Where?"

"To the Spiritualist Church in Singing Creek. Remember, my mom went last Saturday and . . . and she said Bunny was there. So I'm going too to see if she'll speak to us." Already I regretted my choice of subject. All three of my boothmates were staring at me.

"Bunny was *there*?" Roxanne asked. "What does that mean?"

"I'm . . . I'm not sure, but Mom said she knew she was."

"So now you're going too?" Roxanne said. "I thought your mother would go once and see what a scam it was and that would be that."

"That place is loony!" Paul chimed in. "We used to have a neighbor, this old farmer guy with no teeth, and he'd go there every week. He said his dead mother talked to him and told him what crops would be the best to plant and which ones he'd lose money on. And he believed it!"

"It's not just crazy people," I said, but Roxanne wouldn't let me finish a sentence.

"Your father is letting you go? He hates even regular church!"

"He doesn't know I'm going yet."

"God, Liz, he'll have a fit! Just because your mother is having a breakdown over Bunny's death—"

This time I interrupted her. "I don't see why Spiritualism is any crazier than lots of other beliefs. You think God made the earth in six days? You think the Red

Sea parted? You think there was really an ark with two elephants and two giraffes and two bunny rabbits? I'm not saying I believe in Spiritualism, but I think it's possible that people's souls could live on after they die. Why is that more ridiculous than any other belief?"

"Because you can't prove it," she said.

"You can't prove any religion! You just believe it because you want to," I said.

Nathan sat motionless, staring into his Coke. Shit. This obviously wasn't a good subject for him either.

Roxanne shook her head. "You don't really think Bunny is going to *talk* to you. I know why you're doing this," she said.

Where was that duct tape, anyway? "Oh, you do? You've figured out my inner motivations?"

"Yeah. You're trying to get your mother back. I mean, she's been so nuts since Bunny died. You think if you go with her, you can keep her from going totally cuckoo."

"That's not it at all. My mother is not *nuts*! You don't actually know *everything*, Roxanne. I'm going because I think it's interesting, that's all."

Roxy sat back in the booth looking unconvinced.

Nathan cleared his throat. "I should probably be going. I've got my grandmother's car, and—"

"Yeah, me too," I said. "I'm really tired."

"It's not even ten o'clock yet!" Roxanne protested.

"It's been a long day for me," I said. "With the recital and all."

"And the striptease, too," Roxanne said, smirking.

Damn her! Nathan said good-bye to Paul and my ex-best-friend while I headed straight for the door.

We were out of the parking lot before Nathan said, "You know, nobody in the audience could really see anything. You were turned sideways and—"

"Your sister had her hand over your eyes. I think other people could see."

"Well, so what? I mean, it was only your family and a bunch of old folks who'll forget about it by tomorrow."

"And your family, and my wonderful friend Roxanne. *She* won't forget."

"She was just kidding you. You have to let things slide off your back a little bit. I mean, really, in the long run, is this important? No. It's just a dumb thing that happened. Someday it'll probably be a funny story you'll tell people for a laugh."

I couldn't imagine. "Maybe when I'm a hundred and five."

He smiled—his low-key, no-wattage, half smile—but it was nice to see it anyway.

We were almost home when he said, "Are you really going to that church tomorrow?"

"Yeah. I guess you think it's ridiculous too."

He was quiet for a minute, then said, "I don't know what I think. I guess it seems too easy. It would be hard for me to believe my mother could still talk to me after she was . . . you know, gone."

I nodded. "Well, I'm not convinced yet either, but my mother came home so happy after the service last week, I figure it won't hurt to go and see. I don't have anything to lose, right?"

"I guess," he said, shrugging. We pulled into Crabby's driveway. "Anyway, thanks for saving me back there. I don't like to tell too many people about . . . you know . . . my mom. They treat me funny . . . and it's hard enough without that."

"Yeah, that's what I figured," I said. "Besides, you never tell Roxanne anything you don't want the entire Valley to hear about."

"Good to know." We climbed out of the car. "If you want, you can tell me how the church thing goes tomorrow," he said. "I'm kind of interested."

"Sure," I said. "Maybe you can even come along sometime."

"I don't know," he said, as he headed for the porch. "We'll see." Under the porch light his eyes seemed like lava pools, deep and scalding.

Maybe it was just because I was aggravated with Roxanne and anybody would have looked good in comparison, but all of a sudden Nathan seemed like somebody I wanted to get to know. To get to know *well*.

Chapter Nine

Singing Creek was about forty minutes up Route 10 from Tobias. I spent most of the drive replaying my parents' argument in my head. I wasn't sure I'd ever heard either of them that angry before.

"Were you planning to sneak off and not even tell me?" Dad yelled. I was upstairs changing from shorts into jeans, and I stayed up there to wait until the fireworks stopped.

"Actually, yes. If you hadn't come back from the tennis courts so soon, that was exactly what I was planning to do," Mom yelled back. "Because I knew you'd have a ridiculously overdramatic reaction, just like you *are* having."

"Liz is my daughter too, you know. I think I should have some say about whether or not you drag her to this freak show you call a church."

"I'm not *dragging* her. She *wants* to come with me. She wants to contact Bunny. What's so terrible about that?"

"It's terrible to lie to a child. It's terrible to get her hopes up about something that's a complete fabrication."

"Oh, if *you* don't believe it, it must be a lie, is that it? Listen, Jack, just because your father was a hypocrite who stuck his hand in the church till doesn't mean that everyone who believes in something is a liar or a fool!" Wow, Mom was hitting below the belt.

When Dad finally answered her, his voice was low and furious. "All I know is, anyone who says you can talk to dead people is a liar, and anyone who believes it is a fool. In fact, in my book that's the *definition* of a fool."

It went on like that for twenty minutes, until finally I crept downstairs and went out to the car. Mom stormed outside after me, and Dad stood in the doorway glaring at us as we drove away.

Why did people get so crazy about what other people believed? Entire countries fought wars over it. That seemed to be what most wars were fought over—that somebody had different beliefs than you had. It was insane. Couldn't we all just believe what we wanted without forcing everybody else to think the same way? Yelling at people, or *shooting* at them, didn't usually convince them to believe you, anyway.

After Mom calmed down enough to speak to me, she said, "I'm glad you didn't let your father's prejudices change your opinion about Singing Creek."

I didn't really *have* an opinion yet, but I didn't say that. I was happy that Mom wanted me to go with her, and for now that was enough. Still, I hated that my decision had made Dad so angry.

"I wish you and Dad didn't get so mad at each other," I said. "I don't like it when you argue."

She waved away my problem. "Children never do," she said. "But parents are human too. You're getting old enough to understand that, Liz."

I frowned. "No matter how old I am, I'm not going to like hearing you argue," I said.

"Well, if your father refuses to act maturely about this, you'll probably have to hear it again," she said.

It irked me that she put all the blame on Dad—as if it were obvious that she was right and he was wrong—and I thought to myself, Not if I don't go to Singing Creek again, I won't.

We pulled into a small parking lot behind a two-story brown shingled building with the paint peeling off. As soon as I got out of the car, I could hear the creek.

"It's down there," Mom said, pointing through a grove of locust trees. "Can you hear it singing?"

I followed her to a clearing where we could see the stream falling over a series of rock embankments. It was a pretty scene, not unlike hundreds of others in these hills—except for the sound.

"It's more like whistling than singing," I said.

She nodded. "Something to do with the way the rocks are spaced, I think. Apparently the Native Americans who used to live here believed that the souls of their ancestors spoke to them when they came to this spot. They called it Talking Waters. When the Spiritualists came here in the 1930s, they changed it to Singing Creek. It's a thin place, a spot where the barriers between the human world and the spirit world are thin enough that we can see between them. We believe the flowing water is a sort of channel that helps those in the spirit world communicate with us."

"We"? "Us"? Was Mom already a part of this strange world? A few weeks ago she barely knew what a Spiritualist was.

"Hey, Christine! I see you brought a friend."

I turned around to see Monica Winters standing in the parking lot in sweatpants baggy enough to cover two butts the size of hers. If Monica was any indication, the Spiritualists certainly didn't dress up for their services. I guess dead people don't care what you look like.

"Just my daughter," Mom said as I followed her out of the clearing with an arrow stuck in my heart. Why did she say things like that? Okay, I wasn't her best friend, but *just* her daughter? That wasn't the way Bunny had felt about her!

Monica put a hand on my shoulder as we came up to her, but I shrugged it off. "Right!" she said. "It's Liz, isn't it?"

I mumbled a reply, but she wasn't listening, anyway. She

was really only interested in my mother. Monica held Mom's arm as they walked together into the brown building. I followed, although by then I almost wished I hadn't come. I'd gotten Dad all upset over this, and now Mom didn't even seem to care that I was here. Besides, there was something about Monica Winters I didn't like, although I realized that might just be because Mom *did* like her. But Monica was nothing at all like Mom's old friends, who'd obviously been banished, along with Dad, from the world of believers. Would I have to choose one side or the other too?

I followed them up a musty wooden stairway into a big open room that had six or seven pews strewn across it in uneven rows. Behind the pews were a variety of folding chairs and behind those, pushed against the walls, were ancient easy chairs and couches, the kind you usually saw at the dump, the cushions sunken in and the upholstery on the arms worn down to wood.

It was hot up there even though two fans blew from the back of the room toward a small stage with a worn-looking pulpit in the middle. There were about twenty or twenty-five people sitting down already, most of them wearing skimpy summer clothing, although few were young and nobody was as young as I was. A very large woman in a pink tank top and shorts leaned on a cane as she made her way to the front of the room, then sat carefully on a chair next to a harp that she pulled toward herself and began to play.

This place might be called a church, but it was about as much like the Waverly Presbyterian as a mailbox is like the post office. An old *rural* mailbox.

"We're late," Monica whispered. "Let's sit down."

We chose seats in the rear pew, which was still too close to the front for me. Now that I was actually there, the whole idea was starting to seem weird and scary. I glanced around. Who were these people? Most of them were at least middle-aged, although a few twentysomethings were scattered through the crowd. Most of the men had beards, and several had long ponytails hanging down their backs. Most of the women also had long hair, and everyone but Mom and me looked as if they'd chosen their outfits from the racks at the Salvation Army.

Of course, there were lots of people in the Valley who looked like this, people who didn't earn enough money for new clothes, people who wanted to look like struggling artists—and some who really were. People who thought the sixties were just about to make a comeback. But somehow this group seemed different—you had the feeling they didn't even *know* what they looked like. Like they got dressed in the dark, didn't own a mirror, and liked it that way.

A woman with a long gray braid who was wearing overalls walked up to the pulpit and asked us to say the Lord's Prayer. I was surprised by that—it seemed like such a normal church activity.

"That's Reverend Irene," Monica said, leaning over to talk to me. Somehow I'd gotten stuck sitting next to her instead of Mom. "And the man on the straight-backed chair is Reverend Samuel. They're our regular ministers, but other people in the community can do healings and readings too."

I nodded, just to shut her up, but wondered what exactly a "healing" or a "reading" was. Reverend Irene looked like she could probably roll out a decent pie crust with her big puffy fingers, but I couldn't imagine her healing anybody. And Reverend Samuel seemed to already be in the afterlife. Not that he was old. In fact, he seemed pretty young and way too good-looking, with his square jaw and longish black hair, to be hanging around this decrepit group. But when you looked at his face, there didn't seem to be anybody home. His eyes were out of focus and I figured he must already be visiting some world other than this one.

After a creaky chorus of "Amazing Grace" the healing began. Three chairs were set up in the front of the room just below the pulpit, facing away from the congregation. Reverend Irene stood behind one of them, Reverend Samuel behind another, and a man with a white ponytail claimed the third.

"That's Peter Noble," Monica said. "Also known as Running Fox. He's a medium too—he teaches my development group."

Yeah, whatever. I just wanted to get to the part where Bunny could talk to us. But it turned out we all had to go up for a healing if we wanted one of the ministers to give us a reading. "You have to have your energy cleared," Monica explained, "so they can read you."

Energy cleared? No wonder Dad thought this was a bunch of hooey, I thought as I walked up to the front of the room. The healing was painless, although I didn't feel particularly *clear* afterward. I sat in Running Fox's chair. He didn't touch me, but I could tell he was holding his hands a fraction of an inch above my head. He seemed to be making sweeping gestures as if pushing something out of the way. He continued this down the sides of my face and then down my back. All I felt was static electricity. After about five minutes he laid his hands on my shoulders, and when he raised them again, I understood I was finished. As I walked back to the pew, I saw him shake his hands out, as if flinging away whatever cooties he'd picked up from me. Weird.

Mom and Monica got healed too, and when they returned to the pew, I made sure I was next to Mom instead of the whispering Monica.

After singing the "Battle Hymn of the Republic," which Reverend Irene explained was to "get the spirits riled up," the readings began. Reverend Irene went first, calling out to several people in the front row.

"May I come to you?" she asked.

They always answered, "Yes, please."

And then she began to talk, telling them about the vibrations she felt, the letter of a name she saw, the older woman or young child who was trying to come through. She asked the people if they understood what she was saying, and they said, "Yes, yes, my aunt *was* tall," or, "My *dad's* name started with J!"

But the longer I listened, the more disappointed I became. I didn't believe a word she said. Each time she hesitated I knew she was making up what she'd say next. She was a silly old lady on a power trip. Dad was right. I was *so* disappointed. Bunny wouldn't be able to talk to us.

Reverend Irene told Monica that there was a cold breeze surrounding her. There was a small dog and the letter *V* and a blue car, and other mismatched images that sounded more like a segment of *Sesame Street* than communication from the dead. Monica smiled and said she understood and thanked her for the message. What message? Anybody could make up a bunch of nouns and initials.

Reverend Samuel stood up as Reverend Irene sat down, obviously exhausted from her trip to the Other Side. Instead of dressing for a hayride like most of the other people in the room, he wore a black suit and a dark tie. He looked like he was ready to bury the dead, not speak to them. Again, I was riveted by the look on his face—he was not living with the rest of us. He looked around the hall and then pointed to Mom.

"The woman in the white blouse. May I come to you?"

"Yes, please," Mom said excitedly.

He closed his eyes and his hands began to circle in front of him as though he were stirring a bowl with each hand. When he spoke, his words rushed out, uncontrolled, tripping over themselves as though he couldn't have stopped them or edited them even if he'd wanted to.

"There is great warmth and smoke—as if a fireplace or a furnace or a stove—there is a woman from the plane above you—the letter *E*—the letter *L*—she's tall—she holds flowers—there is an old truck in a garage—she wants me to tell you she is happy and she remembers everything—she's hurrying—she always hurries—she sends her love and she says you know that she does. She says also there is love for . . ." And here he finally slowed down, perhaps confused. "Love for someone who is on the plane below you. Perhaps someone who is also here today. Is that correct?"

I looked up at Mom who was standing up, stunned, with tears running down her face. "Yes, yes, that's right. She means my daughter." She put her hand on the back of my head and I felt the weight of it burning into me like a branding iron. At last she was claiming me. "Here! My daughter, Elizabeth!" she cried.

He nodded and looked at me. "Yes, that's right. May I come to you now, Elizabeth?"

Suddenly I felt like the only person in that hot, dusty room—just me and Reverend Samuel and whatever he was looking at over my trembling shoulder.

"Yes, you may," I said, my throat all but closed up. Was Bunny actually asking for me?

Reverend Samuel's eyes closed again and his hands flew in circles. He began to nod. "Yes, she's still there. She is sending you love. She says to tell you that you make beautiful noises, sounds. Perhaps she means an instrument."

Mom's hand, now on my shoulder, dug into my skin and held on tight. "Oh, my God," she said.

A chill ran up my back although it was hot as an oven in that room. How did Reverend Samuel know about my piano playing? My recital? I didn't really believe in this stuff, did I? But sitting there in a roomful of people who *did* believe, I started to think I might be wrong.

Reverend Samuel continued. "There was an accident, with a bus—someone was lost—perhaps not physically lost. Something to do with a bus. Do you understand that?"

For a second I couldn't speak, but Reverend Samuel had his eyes open now and he was staring at me. "No," I said. "Not that part, about the bus."

"You'll understand it later," he said confidently. "She's telling you not to worry. Things will be better for you soon." Then he closed his eyes again and breathed deeply, as if he were taking a break.

"Thank you," Mom said, sinking back into the pew, still crying. He opened his eyes and nodded to her, then began to look over the congregation for another person to read. The readings went on for another half hour or so, but I couldn't concentrate on them and I knew Mom couldn't either. She went through her own handkerchiefs and about ten tissues that Monica handed her. I didn't feel like crying though—I felt like asking a million questions: Did he *see* Bunny? Did he actually hear her speak? How? What did she look like? Where *was* she? I was so confused. I didn't know what had just happened or what I believed anymore. But I knew I wanted more messages from Bunny.

The service finally ended with more harp playing, and we stood up. Monica leaned across Mom and said, "So, what did you think?" Somehow, hearing Monica's eager voice woke me up from the trance of Reverend Samuel's reading.

Mom answered for me. "That man is a genius! He spoke to her. He really spoke to Bunny!" She turned to me. "You realize she was at your concert, Liz. Bunny heard you play!"

I nodded and smiled. I wanted to believe that Bunny could hear me playing the piano, and that she sent me her love, but there was still a part of me that couldn't buy it. After all, I was sure that Reverend Irene was a big fake. Were some of the ministers for real and others not? That didn't make sense.

Besides, if Bunny had been at my concert, wouldn't she have made some reference to my blouse coming open? Then I'd *really* believe she'd been there. Or couldn't dead people make jokes?

Reverend Irene announced that there were coffee and

doughnuts in the fellowship hall downstairs and we should all adjourn there for sugar and caffeine, but I really wanted to get outside, to breathe air that wasn't stuffed with ghosts and lies and maybe even some weird truths.

Monica was headed downstairs and Mom would have followed her, but I pulled her back.

"Can we just go home? Please? I want to . . . I need to get out," I said.

"It's overwhelming, isn't it?" Mom said. "I know." She called down to Monica and said we were leaving but she'd call her later. Obviously, Monica was her new best friend.

Once we got outside, I took a deep breath and tried to unscramble my mind. I could hear the whistling creek, *the thin place,* burbling over the rocks. Was it really magical? How could I believe what I'd just been told? But how could I *not* believe it? It would be wonderful to believe it!

If only there were some way to *prove* it, to make sure the ministers weren't making the whole thing up. Of course, if you could prove it, it probably wouldn't be a religion. Religions were all about things you couldn't prove. If you could just chat with your dead relatives whenever you wanted to, people would't get so hyped up about it.

Now that I was outside, away from Reverend Samuel's staring eyes and whirling hands, I was amazed at myself. Because for a few minutes there, I'd believed him. I'd really believed him. And maybe I still did. It occurred to me that I might have believed him even if he hadn't said that about

Bunny hearing my music. I might have believed almost anything he told me—at least while I was inside the church, under his spell—because I *wanted* to believe that Bunny could still see me and hear me and talk to me, even though my brain told me that was impossible. My poor brain, which felt close to exploding with confusion.

In the car Mom blew her nose again, then backed out of the space. "So," she said. "Pretty amazing, isn't it?"

I nodded.

"What are you going to say to Dad? You want to come with me again, don't you?"

Did I? "I guess so," I said. "It's a little . . . scary." But "scary" wasn't really the right word. "Shocking," "disturbing," "spooky" were closer, but not entirely right either. I felt simultaneously as if I were being taken in, made a fool of by a bunch of crackpots, and also as if I were walking through doors I wasn't meant to enter, learning things I shouldn't know.

"Don't tell your father it scared you," Mom said. "He'll have a fit."

I couldn't imagine *what* I'd tell my father. "Maybe not scared," I said. "Just confused. When they say stuff that doesn't make sense to you—like about the truck in the garage and the bus accident—I mean, if some of what they say is wrong, does that mean the whole thing—"

"Oh, no," Mom said. "Monica has explained a lot of this to me. She says often you won't completely understand the whole reading. The mediums are getting images and they don't always read them correctly. You take what you understand."

"But what if they goofed up the whole thing? What if they aren't any good? What if they're just making it all—"

She glanced over at me. "Do you really think Reverend Samuel could have made that all up? About the smoky furnace, which was obviously my kiln, the first two letters of her name, hearing your piano recital? Could that all be coincidental?"

"But how do we know for sure that he was talking to—"

"I can't believe you aren't convinced, Liz. What more do you need to see?"

"I'm not saying I *don't* believe it. But you have to admit, it's pretty weird—that minister with the black suit and the dark eyes and the—"

"I'm surprised at you, Liz. You're being so judgmental. Reverend Samuel is totally committed to his work." I wondered if he'd ever been committed to anything else. "Monica says you need to open your heart."

"She said that about *me*?"

"All of us. She says we have to let the spirits come to us. Be open to them. Be willing to take what they have to give us."

I wasn't sure I wanted what they had to give me. I closed my eyes and Mom stopped talking, which good because I couldn't listen to her anymore if she wasn't going to listen to me back. Bunny had already given me a lot while she was alive. It was great that she might still be listening to my piano recitals, but in a way I already knew that. Not that I knew she was "out there" somewhere actually listening, but she was always with me when I played the piano—she always would be. I wasn't sure I needed her to be looking down on me from above, or tuned in to me on some spiritual radio station.

Bunny had always been tuned in to me. It was my mother who was on another wavelength.

Chapter Ten

By the time I got out of bed Sunday morning, Dad was holed up in his office with the door closed, which obviously meant he didn't want to talk about Spiritualism anymore. The night before, he'd listened tight-lipped to Mom's enthusiastic story of our encounter with Reverend Samuel and the spirit world. He didn't get angry and he didn't ask any questions, but he kept glancing over at me as if he were waiting for me to give him a different version of events. But I couldn't. Mom was telling him the truth. Whether or not Bunny had really communicated with us I wasn't sure, but something remarkable seemed to have happened in that rickety brown building. And Dad was not happy to hear it.

Mom, on the other hand, seemed almost back to normal. Not only was she in her studio at nine o'clock on

Sunday morning, but the open-studio sign was already out and she was busy wedging a new batch of clay, which meant she intended to work. National Public Radio was filling her in on the news of the week, and she had to turn it down to talk to me.

"Hey," she said. "You're finally up."

I'm finally up? She was the one who'd barely gotten out of bed for weeks!

"Do you want me to help you with customers today?" I asked.

"You don't need to," she said. "I don't mind stopping work to make a few bucks." She actually sounded happy. "Oh, Lily's little girl was over here looking for you. Courtney. She's such a doll. I think she was hoping you'd hang around with her today. She's probably kind of lonely."

"Do you think . . . you know, that they've told her . . . about her mother?"

"Oh no, I don't think so. Lily's been feeling much better since she got out of the hospital last week. I don't think she wants to tell Courtney until . . . well, until she has to."

"But what if she finds out some other way? Or what if Lily gets sick again really quickly—"

"Who knows?" Mom said, turning back to the mound of clay. "Maybe Lily will get well and then she won't have to tell Courtney at all. Miracles do happen!"

I didn't think Nathan would have announced to me that his mother was dying if there was any chance for a miraculous recovery. But Mom seemed willing to believe *anything* now. Anything that would keep her from facing the truth. Or maybe she was right and I was being cynical. After all, I had been willing to believe in miracles for at least a few minutes when Reverend Samuel went into his arm-waving trance and told me that Bunny had heard my recital.

I could see Courtney out on her grandmother's porch with her Barbies again. I didn't mind spending time with her, but I didn't really want to stuff a plastic doll into tight polyester all day.

"Maybe I'll take Courtney to the lake, if Mrs. Crosby says it's okay. She probably hasn't been down there yet."

"That's a good idea. Maybe Nathan would like to go with you too."

"I don't know. He and Courtney argue a lot. He probably wouldn't want to."

"Well, you could *ask* him anyway!" she said with a little laugh.

Could she be more transparent? Okay, I was almost sixteen and had never had a boyfriend, but did she think a furious, depressed guy whose mother was dying was really a hot prospect? True, I was interested in him myself, but I certainly wasn't expecting anything in return.

I decided before going over to Crabby's house, I'd play the piano for half an hour. Mozart was just what I needed to put Dad's anger and Mom's weirdness and Courtney's troubles right out of my head. I could have happily spent the whole morning on the piano bench, but somehow Courtney and her motley bunch of Barbies wormed their way into my consciousness, so I gave up and went across the street.

Courtney was excited about going to the lake, although she probably would have been happy to go anywhere to get away from that house.

"Can we take your dogs, too? They're so cute! I always wanted a dog!"

"Sure, they love the lake. But we need to ask your grandma if it's okay first."

"We can ask my *mother.* She'll let me go."

Sure enough, Lily was sitting up in the living room, reading a book. She was very pale, but she smiled when she heard my plan. "That sounds great! I always loved going to the lake when I was a kid. Do they still have a float anchored way out that you can swim to?"

I nodded. "But you have to be at least twelve and a good swimmer to go out. The lifeguard keeps track."

"Well, I should hope so!" Mrs. Crosby had come into the room to give us her opinion. "There was a boy drowned in that lake, you know."

"Mom, that was years ago. *I* was a kid when that happened," Lily said.

"Anything can happen any time. Water is dangerous," Crabby said.

Lily rolled her eyes. "It's perfectly safe. The swimming area is roped off and there's a lifeguard on duty, right Liz?"

"Yeah. I've never heard of anybody drowning there."

"Well, there was a boy," Mrs. Crosby grumbled. "I remember."

"Maybe Nathan would like to go with you," Lily said.

God, was this a conspiracy? I hoped he wouldn't think it was *my* idea to ask him.

"Sure," I said, shrugging, as if it were no big deal one way or the other.

"Oh, does he have to?" Courtney said, her mouth turning down at the corners. She grabbed on to my arm. "I want to go with Liz by myself."

"I think it's a good idea," Mrs. Crosby said. "Get that mopey kid out of his room. Besides, he's bigger than you two girls, if something happens. I assume he knows how to swim."

"Yes, mother, he knows how to swim. We lived on Cape Cod. Both my children know how to swim." Lily called his name a few times, and Nathan appeared at the top of the stairs. Courtney stamped her foot but didn't say anything.

"Liz is taking Courtney down to the lake to swim. Do you want to go with them?" Lily asked.

Nathan looked at me as if asking my permission. On the one hand I wanted him to come, but the idea of spending hours with him, making conversation and eating lunch and everything, made me feel slightly sick.

"Yeah," I said. "You should come. The lake's really pretty."

He nodded without smiling. "Okay. Why not?"

I went back home to put on my suit and get towels and sunblock. I stood in front of the mirror in my room for about ten minutes staring at myself in my one-piece swimming suit. Most of the other teenage girls at the lake wore bikinis, but I'd never liked showing off my body like that. Not that my body was bad or anything—and this year it actually had some curves to it. But I saw the way boys looked at the bikini-clad girls, and I knew I wouldn't be able to stand it. I would be so embarrassed! And what if your top came loose while you were swimming? No, give me my racer-back Speedo, thank you.

But as I stood there looking at myself, trying to figure out what I really looked like and failing, I wondered if Nathan would spend the day staring at the bikini wearers. Well, if he did, he did. There was nothing I could do about it.

I put my shorts and T-shirt back on over my suit and threw some apples and dog biscuits into my bag, then called Woody and Pete. They were all excited to be going somewhere and danced around so much it took me forever to get their leashes on them. Courtney came running up the lawn with Nathan plodding behind her.

"Can I take one of the dogs?" she asked.

"Sure. Take Pete. He's not as big as Woody."

Nathan was lugging a large canvas bag.

"What's in there?" I asked.

"My grandmother made me bring it. It's leftover fried chicken from last night and about two tons of other stuff."

"Really? Crab—I mean . . ." I glanced at Courtney, but she was too interested in Pete to be paying attention. "She packed us a picnic?"

Nathan shrugged. "Sometimes she does a normal thing when you don't expect it. But then she's meaner than hell for the next two days just so you don't get the idea she actually likes you or anything."

It's only a ten minute walk from our house to the lake, but when you don't know what to say to somebody, it seems like an hour. At least with Courtney there we could talk to her and to the dogs instead of each other. She was such a happy kid, which made me think how awful it was going to be when she found out about her mother. I wondered if Nathan was thinking the same thing.

The lake wasn't crowded yet—most people were probably still at church. We found a good spot on the sand near enough to some trees that I could tie Pete and Woody up after their swim so they wouldn't wander off. As soon as they saw the water, they started pulling on their leashes, and Pete almost dragged Courtney in. The dogs couldn't swim in the roped-off area, but Courtney was happy to throw sticks into the lake for them to retrieve, and that kept all three of them busy.

Nathan and I spread our towels out and he stripped off his T-shirt while I pretended to have something more important to do than stare at him.

"You coming in?" he asked.

"I will later," I said, trying to imagine how I was going to get out of my clothes in front of Nathan without turning twelve shades of red.

I watched him run into the water and swim out to the rope boundary, then dive under it and continue out to the anchored float. His stroke was strong and he covered the distance in a few minutes. He climbed up onto the float. Even from shore I could see he had muscles.

I decided it would be better to get out of my clothes while he was far away. By the time he dove back into the water and swam to shore, I was sitting primly, hugging my knees to my chin.

Nathan flung some water at me as he dropped to his towel.

"Ahh! It's cold!" I yelled.

He laughed and I got a glimpse of what he must have been like . . . before. "Cold? You think *this* is cold? This is a bathtub compared to the outer beaches on the Cape. The Atlantic never warms up that far north, but I like it cold. It makes you feel alive." And just that quickly he was reminded of his life, and the smile collapsed in on itself.

"I'd like to go to Cape Cod sometime," I said, hoping to get him over the awkward moment. "I haven't been that many places, but I want to travel someday. I'm babysitting for a family this summer, and I'm saving everything I make so I can take a trip somewhere. I don't know where I'll go yet, but . . ." I ran out of words, but he didn't seem to be listening, anyway.

Just to be doing something, I rooted through my bag for a hair elastic and pulled my mane back. I was just about to get up and run for the lake when he spoke.

"So, did you go to that Spiritualist place yesterday?"

"Uh-huh."

He was picking up handfuls of sand and letting it pour through his fingers. "What was it like?"

I settled back on the sand and tried to figure out how to explain it. "Well, it was a little strange. Kind of intense."

"How? You mean, the people were intense?"

I nodded. "One of the ministers—I guess that's what they call them—Reverend Samuel, he kind of creeped me out. But then, well, it seemed like he might really have been talking to Bunny, my grandmother."

Nathan looked up sharply. "Really? You think he really was?"

I grimaced. "It's hard to know. Some of the stuff that went on at the church I couldn't buy at all, but then when he started to talk to Mom and me, he said a lot of things that rang true."

"Like what?"

"Well, first he said he felt 'a great warmth' like a smoky furnace, or something like that, and Mom thought that meant her kiln in her studio. Which it could. She and Bunny spent so much time together in there."

He grunted. "Maybe, but 'a great warmth' could mean something to almost anybody. It could mean they had a fireplace, or they lived in Florida or something."

"I know, but that wasn't all. He gave the letters *E* and *L,* for Elizabeth—"

"Except you said everybody called her Bunny. Shouldn't he have gotten the letters *B* and *U*?" He shook his head as though discounting everything I was saying.

"I'm just telling you what happened. He said she was 'from the plane above you,' which Mom said means the generation before you. He said she was tall and she always hurried, which is true—"

"Again, how many people could that apply to?"

"Well, wait. The most amazing thing was what he told *me.* He said she had a message for someone on the plane below my mother, which would be me. And then he said that she told him I made beautiful sounds. He thought she meant on an instrument." Even repeating it made me shiver. "As if she'd been listening to me play the piano."

Nathan was quiet for a minute. "Huh. That is kind of amazing, when you put it all together. You think she was listening to your recital?"

"That's what it sounds like, doesn't it?"

"Did he say anything else?"

"He did, but the rest of it didn't make as much sense," I admitted. "There was something about a truck in a garage, and flowers, and a bus accident. I didn't understand any of that, but he told me I would understand it later. Mom says they always say that, as if they're predicting the future or something."

He'd stopped playing with the sand and was staring at me now. "I don't believe anybody can predict the future. Does your mom really believe all this stuff?"

"I think she does."

"Do you?"

I looked over to where Courtney was jumping around with the dogs, all three of them soaked already. "I believed it while he was talking." Nathan would think I was crazy now. "I don't know. I think it would be kind of nice to believe it. I wish Bunny *could* have heard my recital."

"Sure, but wanting something to be true doesn't make it true. Besides, what if . . . ," Nathan began, then scowled and tried again. "What if somebody you knew died and you *didn't* want them watching you forever? I mean, that would be sort of creepy, wouldn't it?"

I shrugged. "I don't know that many people who've died."

He was silent for several minutes and I thought he'd let the topic drop, but then he said, "My dad is dead. I wouldn't want *him* spying on me."

Lord! I didn't know what to say to that—first his dad died and now his mother was going to? How unfair!

I guess he knew what I was thinking. He shrugged. "Mom was already divorced from him when he died. We hadn't seen him in years. I don't think Courtney even remembers what he looked like. He was a drunk—he drove off the road. At least he didn't kill anybody else. It wasn't a big deal when he died or anything. I mean, not like, you know . . ."

I knew. But still. I'd hardly known anybody who'd had even one parent die, much less two. It was obviously impossible not to feel bad for Nathan. And for Courtney! I looked over at her again and it killed me how happy she looked.

"That's terrible!" I said. "First your dad and now . . ." If he couldn't say the words, how could I?

He nodded, following my gaze over to his sister. "Especially for her. I mean, I'm practically grown-up, but she's still a kid." His voice was a little shaky, and he turned his face down to the sand. Sixteen was not *that* grown-up. He cleared his throat, then said, "Mom can't bear to tell her, but if she doesn't do it pretty soon, I think old Crabby will do it for her."

"She wouldn't, would she?"

"I don't know what she'd do. She's a crazy old bat."

I had a sudden realization, but I didn't know how to ask about it. "Did you come here so that . . . I mean, would you and Courtney have to . . . to live with her . . . after?"

He'd picked up a rock while we were talking, and now he pitched it with such force that it ricocheted off a pine tree and flew into the lake, fortunately not near any swimmers. "No!" he said, jumping to his feet. "We can't! Mom thinks we can, but it isn't happening. I don't know where we'll go, but we can't stay here. We'll go back to the Cape and I'll get a job or something. I can wait tables at the place Mom worked. I can . . . I don't know . . . I'll figure something out, but *I will not stay with her.*"

I stood up too, because I felt like I should stay with him. My question had opened Pandora's box and his anger had leaped out uncontrollably. I felt like I ought to try to help him come up with a plan. After all, *nobody* could live with *her.* Didn't his mother know that? She hadn't been able to live there herself!

"Maybe I can help you figure out—," I began.

His face was twisted with pain. "I don't want to talk about it anymore," he said. "You can't help me. Nobody can." And with that he raced toward the water and jumped in. I followed him, but it took me a minute to get used to the cold, and by the time I started swimming he was already under the rope and going toward the float. I swam behind him but couldn't catch up. When I crawled out of the water onto the platform, he was already diving off of it, heading back to shore. I had to rest before I could follow him, or he'd know another dead person.

When I joined them fifteen minutes later, Nathan and Courtney were spreading food out on our towels. Nathan had tied the dogs to a tree, and Courtney had given them some biscuits so they wouldn't bark.

"Look at all the stuff Gramma sent us to eat!" Courtney cried. "There's chicken and potato salad and beans. And look! There's even cake!"

"Calm down, Courtney," Nathan said. A sour look stuck to his face. "You act like you've never had food before. And anyway, good old *'Gramma'* probably just wanted to get rid of this stuff. We'll probably all get ptomaine poisoning from it."

Courtney stuck her tongue out at her brother. "You're mean. I love Gramma's potato salad. She makes it even better than Mom does."

"She does not!" Nathan said. "And how can you call her 'Gramma,' anyway? Like you've known her your whole life!"

"I like having a gramma," Courtney said. "We never had one before. Even if she does yell sometimes. She's nice, too."

"That's news to me," Nathan said.

"She probably just doesn't know how to be nice to kids," Courtney said. "Since she never had any."

"*Mom* is her child, stupid," Nathan said.

"Nathan!" I said. "Don't call your sister stupid!" He was in a terrible mood, and poor Courtney was taking the brunt of it. I wished we'd never had that talk.

But Courtney wasn't about to let Nathan step on her tail. "Yeah, don't call me stupid, stupid," she said. "Anyhow, I *know* Mom is her child. I meant, she never had any *grand*children."

"Whatever." Nathan grabbed a piece of chicken and turned his back on us. For Courtney's sake I tried to pretend I was enjoying our picnic, but I felt awful about all the things Nathan had told me. No wonder he always looked so miserable.

When we were done eating, Nathan started to pack the food back into the canvas bag. "I'm going back home," he said. "I'll take the food. You don't mind staying with Courtney by yourself, do you?" he asked me.

"No, not at all," I said. But I was disappointed that we wouldn't have another chance to talk, to straighten things out, maybe figure out a plan. It felt like he was running away from me.

"Yeah!" Courtney yelled. "We can be alone, Liz!"

I watched Nathan hike down the path away from the lake, his shoulders drooping. I had to do something to help him!

But at the moment, I belonged to Courtney who had grabbed my hand to drag me to my feet.

"You're my best friend, Liz! Let's go play with the dogs again! Let's get wet! I wish you were my sister!"

Chapter Eleven

Do you like it?"

Mom had just presented me with a box from Lord & Taylor that, when opened, revealed a long-sleeved white blouse festooned with enough ruffles to pass as kitchen curtains.

"You went to the mall," I said, stalling.

She nodded. "I went yesterday with Monica. I decided she had to get some clothes that were made this century."

Great. Not only had she not asked me to go with her to buy my new blouse, but she'd gone with the ever-present Monica and my clothing requirement had obviously been an afterthought. Still, she'd remembered that I needed the blouse—I'd have to give her points for effort. And she was certainly excited about her choice.

"Go try it on," she said, grinning.

I'd been playing the piano and didn't really want to stop, but I took the box upstairs and lifted out the silky blouse. The material felt nice as I pulled the sleeves over my arms, and it was the right size—no gaping when I buttoned it up. Tentatively I turned and looked into the mirror.

Okay, no way on earth was I ever being seen in public in that blouse. Not that it wouldn't look fine on *somebody*— maybe Carlin with her sweet femininity—but it made me look like a large meringue cookie. There were ruffles on the wrists, ruffles down the front, and even ruffles around the neck, which got all caught up in my ruffled hair. The whole effect was ludicrous.

Mom came into my room, still beaming. "It's beautiful, isn't it? You needed something dressier than those plain shirtwaist blouses you've had."

"It's a pretty blouse," I began, "but I'm not sure I'm the kind of person to wear it, you know?" I so much didn't want to hurt her feelings when she'd actually done a somewhat motherly thing.

"Of course you are, Liz! It's time you grew out of your shyness. If you're performing, you should look like a performer! This blouse says, 'Hello, World! Here I am!'"

I was thinking it said something more along the lines of, *Hello, World, I'm a recently groomed standard poodle!* I held out my arms and the ruffles fell over my knuckles. "See, I'm just afraid the sleeves would get in the way when I'm playing," I said.

Mom pushed the sleeves back a little. "Oh, I don't think—"

"And the ruffles here," I said, brushing the layer that covered my chest. "I think they're sort of big for me. I mean, they stick out—"

"Okay, I get it," she said, her face icing over. "You don't like it. Take it off. I'll return it."

Why did everything have to be so difficult with her? A blouse wasn't just a blouse—it was a *test*. Did I love her enough? Did she love me? And there was never a simple answer.

"It's not that I don't *like* it. I just . . . it's not me," I finished lamely.

She sighed. "I've always thought I had a pretty good sense of style. . . ."

"You do!" I said. "But maybe next time I could go with you when you shop."

That was obviously a novel idea to her. "Well, you know, I don't go shopping very often, which is why I was glad to find this pretty blouse."

"Thanks, Mom. Really, I appreciate it, but . . ." I handed the poodle-meringue-curtains back to her.

She shrugged. "To each her own," she said, folding her gift and slipping it back between the tissue paper sheets in the box.

When she walked out of my room, I wondered whether she was thinking that *she'd* failed or I had.

. . .

I didn't see Nathan again all week. I was busy at the Romanows' most of the time, and I assumed he was either moping at Crabby's house or she was keeping him busy getting rid of the twenty years' worth of weeds in her yard.

I asked Mrs. Romanow if she'd mind if I brought Courtney along sometimes when I babysat. Without giving too many details, I said that Courtney's mother was sick and she didn't know anybody but me in Tobias. Mrs. Romanow was sympathetic, but I had to assure her that I wouldn't overlook my responsibilities to her children.

Courtney was thrilled, of course, and came with me on Wednesday. And at first I thought things were going to work out fine. Courtney wanted to "help" me babysit and she did for a while. She poured the drinks while I made sandwiches for lunch. She held Jake's hand when we walked to the swing set in the park, and she pushed him while I pushed Emma. She seemed to be enjoying being a big kid, I thought, but suddenly that changed. I guess I should have seen it coming.

I asked the twins if they wanted to have a piano lesson and they did. As usual they both sat on the bench and I stood behind them.

"I want to learn too!" Courtney said. "Please? I never get to take any lessons!"

I tried to explain to her that I couldn't teach her while we were at the Romanows' but I'd be glad to give her lessons some other time, at my house. I thought she understood me, but then she pulled up a dining-room chair next to the piano bench and started trying to play. It was hard enough to get the twins to pay attention to me—they mostly wanted to bang on the keys and push each other around on the bench. Adding another person to the mix just made things worse.

When Courtney got in her way, Emma started to whine. "You go away," she ordered Courtney. "You're too big." I knew if Mrs. Romanow heard about this, it could screw up my lucrative job.

"Courtney," I said sternly, "you can't sit at the piano now. I'm teaching Emma and Jake."

"I'm just watching," she said. "I'm *helping* them."

"No, you're not!" Emma said. "You're bumping me!"

"Well, if you'd scoot over a little bit—" Courtney complained.

"Courtney, listen to me!" I said. "You can't play piano here. I'll give you lessons another time if you want me to." I hoisted her off the chair and moved it back to the table.

She gave me a look of betrayal that made my heart stop. Why couldn't I give her piano lessons right now? Did Emma and Jake really need to learn to play an instrument this summer? Not as much as Courtney did. Courtney needed all the attention and affection she could get, and I was denying it to her. But this was my *job*.

She put her hands on her hips and her chin quivered. "Then I'm going home!" she said. "I don't like it here."

"You go home!" Emma echoed her.

"No, wait," I said, grabbing her arm. "You can't walk home by yourself. You don't even know how to get there."

"Do you think I'm stupid?" she said. "I walked *here,* didn't I? I can walk home." She jerked away from me and headed for the door.

"Courtney! Please don't leave. I'm in charge of you for the afternoon."

"You aren't in charge of me," she said. "*I'm* in charge of me." And then she banged out the screen door and ran down the street. I called after her, but I knew she wouldn't come back. She was related to Nathan, after all.

I looked up Mrs. Crosby's number in the phone book and dialed, hoping that either Nathan or Lily would answer, but I was out of luck.

"Hullo." It was Crabby herself.

"Hi, Mrs. Crosby. It's, um, Liz. From across the street. Um, Courtney was with me this afternoon, and, um—"

"What happened? Where is she? Did you go to that lake again?"

"No, no. She came with me to my babysitting job. But she decided she wanted to go home, and I couldn't stop her. It's not that far—I'm up on Lake Ridge Road—but I'm not sure she knows the way back by herself. I wanted to let you know—"

"I'll send the boy out to look for her. That all you wanted?"

The boy? "Well, would you call me back and let me know when she gets there?" I asked.

She grunted. "Kind of a worrywart, are ya?"

Me? She was the one who thought Courtney was going to drown every time she got near a puddle. I gave her the number and hung up, hoping Nathan would make the next call. But within ten minutes Crabby called back herself. "She's here. You can relax."

"Oh, great," I said. "Thanks for—" But she was gone already. No details, no *Thanks for letting us know,* nothing. How could Nathan and Courtney possibly live with this woman?

I didn't see Courtney for several days after that. She wasn't playing outside, and I didn't want to go over there and have to talk to Nathan, or worse, his grandmother. How had I gotten so mixed up with these people, anyway?

Friday I got a call from Roxanne. I hadn't spoken to her since the week before when she'd made that "striptease" remark in front of Nathan, but I knew she'd forgotten about it the moment it was out of her mouth, so I followed Nathan's advice and tried to let it roll off my back. Besides, I didn't have enough friends to give one up that easily.

"Are you calling from work?" I asked.

"Yeah. The boss likes me. I can get away with it," she said. "So, do you want to hang out tomorrow?"

"Aren't you hanging out with Paul?"

She sighed. "He's on that damn basketball team and they've got a game tomorrow afternoon. I thought maybe we could go into Waverly on the bus and have lunch, and then come back for the end of the game. We don't have to watch the whole thing."

"Why would I want to watch *any* of it?" I asked.

"Well, Nathan's on the team. Does that make you want to watch it?"

"He *is*? Since when?" Roxanne always found out everything before I did.

"Since Monday. He walked by while the guys were practicing, and Paul talked him into it. Haven't you seen him this week?"

"*No.* Just because he lives across the street from me doesn't mean I keep track of every moves he makes." I knew I sounded madder than I ought to.

"Oh, excuse me," Roxy said. "I thought maybe you liked him. But if you don't, you don't have to go to the game. You can go home when we get back from Waverly."

"What time do you think we'd get back?" I asked. Mom left the house at two fifteen to get to Singing Creek by three, and I knew she expected me to go with her.

"I don't know. Three, maybe after. I want to get a new pair of flip-flops, and maybe go to Used Tunes, too."

Roxanne and I hadn't had a day to just hang out in Waverly in ages, and I loved the used-CD store. It also occurred to me that this was a good excuse *not* to go with Mom. All week I'd been thinking about the "messages" we'd gotten, whether they could possibly have been from Bunny or not. I kept seeing Reverend Samuel's hands twirling around in circles and his long-lost eyes staring into the air. Part of me wanted to go again, to hear what he'd say next time, but another part of me wondered if Dad was right, that Reverend Samuel was a phony who was fooling us all. Since I couldn't figure out what to believe anyway, maybe it would be easier to just avoid it.

"Okay, I'll go," I told Roxanne. "Meet me at the bus stop at ten thirty?"

"Let's make it eleven," she said. "It's Saturday. I need my rest."

"You're not *going* with me? Why on earth not? Bunny *spoke* to you!" Mom was more than a little upset at my disloyalty. It occurred to me too late that I should have told her when we were alone instead of in the kitchen with Dad right there. He couldn't keep a smile off his face.

"It's her decision, Christine," he said. "That's what you told me last week. She gets to make up her own mind."

"It's not like I'm never going again," I said, backpedaling. "I'll go next week, I promise. But I want to hang out with Roxanne tomorrow. I don't want to give up every Saturday to go to Singing Creek."

Mom glared at me and I had to look away. I hated

making her angry. "I don't think of it as *giving up* a day. I think of it as a privilege to be able to speak to your grandmother."

"Oh, for God's sake, Christine," Dad said. He got up from the table and took his plate and mine to the sink. "Liz is fifteen. You can't blame her for not wanting to spend her weekends in that crazy church!"

"I didn't say it was crazy . . . ," I said.

"She's almost sixteen, and I don't see what her age has to do with it, anyway." Mom crumpled up her paper napkin and hurled it in the direction of the trash can, but it missed by a mile. "If she really loved Bunny—"

"Don't go there!" Dad yelled. "Don't you dare try to make Liz feel guilty about this! You know she loved Bunny—you *know* that!"

I could have hugged Dad for defending me. Mom saying that I didn't love Bunny enough made me want to cry.

"Fine," Mom said, bringing her own plate to the sink and dumping it noisily on top of the others. "I'll go alone. I wouldn't want to hinder your social life." She gave me a scorching glance and stalked out to her studio.

"Don't let Mom get to you," Dad said. "You know how emotional she can be. Sometimes I just want to shake some sense into her." I knew he felt sorry for me, but I couldn't look at him. I felt like the two of them were trying to pull me apart and I didn't want to go with either one of them.

"Don't you think there's a chance that Mom could be right about Singing Creek?" I said. "I mean, is it really any crazier than any other religion?"

"Honey," he said, sinking into a chair, "this whole religion question is something you have to decide for yourself. I just don't want you to be taken in by a lot of pious talk or so-called miracle workers. Churches are full of hypocrites who make fools out of needy people. They tell you religion is about praising God and doing good for others, and then they turn around and use it as a reason to condemn people who're different from them. I don't trust any organized religious group, Lizzie. And especially not one that purports to speak to the dead. It can't happen."

"You weren't there," I said quietly.

He sighed deeply. "No, I wasn't. And I won't ever be there. I'm sorry, Liz."

"Well, what *do* you believe in, then?" I asked him.

He studied his fingernails before he answered me. "If I believe in anything, it would be nature—trees, clouds, rain—the life cycles that begin and end, season after season. That makes sense to me—nature as God."

I thought about that. "But that's sort of like the story of the Resurrection, isn't it? I mean, we celebrate Easter in the spring when nature is all coming back to life again."

Dad smiled. "And which do you think came first, the seasons changing or the story of the Resurrection?"

"Okay, but I still don't think that everybody who

believes in God instead of *rain* is a fool or a hypocrite. Bunny wasn't!"

He nodded. "That's true. Bunny was a good soul and a strong believer. But she would have been that way whether she went to church or not, wouldn't she? Church doesn't make you a better person."

I flopped down into the chair next to his. "Mom misses Bunny so much," I said. "She just wants to talk to her again."

Dad reached over and took my hand. "I know that."

"And I do too. I miss Bunny!"

"I know, sweetheart. I miss her too."

"Well then, why can't we *try* to find her again? We aren't hurting anybody by trying!"

"You could hurt yourselves—that's what I'm afraid of," Dad said sadly. "And Lizzie, I don't want to lose you, too."

Lose me *too*? Did he think he'd already lost Mom? I closed my eyes and hummed a little Mozart to scare away that depressing thought.

Roxy and I had a great time in Waverly on Saturday, just like we used to. We spent an hour in Used Tunes, comparing finds, then had lunch at our favorite deli. After that we both got new flip-flops at this funky little store called Stuff, and we still had time for an ice cream from The Cold Cow before we caught the bus back to Tobias.

We spent too much time dissecting Roxanne's

relationship with Paul, the big question being whether or not she should sleep with him. But I tried to be helpful to her and not just the grouch I usually am when she wants to discuss her sex life.

"We've been going together for almost a year already," she said. "Isn't that amazing? It doesn't seem that long."

It seemed much longer to me, but I didn't say so.

"And you know how guys are." I didn't. "They *always* want sex. And it's not that I don't. It's just, you know, a little scary."

"So, do you talk about it with him?" I asked.

She snorted. "Do we talk about anything *else*? Part of me feels like we might as well just do it so we can stop talking about it!"

"What does the other part think?"

She shrugged. "I don't know. I mean, I really like Paul and everything, but I don't think I love him. You know? And everybody always says how it's so much better when you love the person. And I want the first time to be special." She threw out her hands. "But, Lord, it could be *years* before I love anybody!"

I had to laugh. "That would be terrible! Just think! A virgin at eighteen . . . or twenty!"

She laughed too. "No, really, Lizzie. Don't you sometimes feel like virginity is a curse? It's like you haven't passed some big test that you need to pass before you can grow up, only you can't study for it, and you can't even *take* the damn test unless some guy asks you to. Ugh. Sometimes I just want to get it over with."

The only way I could help Roxy was to listen, which, fortunately, was all she really wanted me to do. My experience with boys was limited to a sixth-grade crush who kissed me on the cheek before he moved to Colorado and a guy who stole my pencils in math class every day of seventh grade. At the time, Roxanne assured me this was adoration, but I still think the guy just forgot to bring his own pencils. That was it. Except for Nathan, of course. And girls were the last thing on his mind.

By the time we were on the bus back to Tobias, Roxanne had finally gotten tired of talking about Paul. "Hey, I forgot to ask you," she said, "did you go with your mom to that Spiritualist church last week?"

Damn. I really didn't want to talk to Roxy about that. It was confusing enough trying to figure out what I thought about it without her making jokes. But I had to tell her something.

"I went. It was interesting."

"Really?" She sat forward. "Did they talk to dead people? Did they roll on the floor?"

"Roxy, there's no floor-rolling in the Spiritualist Church. I don't know where you heard that."

"But they do talk to dead people, right?"

I sighed. "They communicate with the spirit world."

"How is that different from talking to dead people?"

"Well, for one thing, it's not like watching a horror movie. It's very quiet and civilized."

"So?" I was clearly not giving her enough information.

"So, what?"

"So, did you talk to . . . communicate with Bunny?"

"Actually, yeah, I think we might have."

Roxanne's eyes widened. "Really? What did she say?"

I shrugged. "A bunch of stuff. About Mom's studio and about my recital. We think . . . I mean, it seemed like she was saying that she'd heard me play the piano."

"No shit! That's awesome! Do you believe it? I mean, maybe somebody told them about it or something."

I really didn't want to get into this with Roxy. She wanted a yes or no answer. True or false. I hadn't made up my mind yet. "I don't think anybody told them, but I don't know if I totally believe it either. I mean, the stuff they say is kind of general. You could interpret it different ways."

"So, it's a hoax?"

"No, I'm not saying that! Roxy, I don't really know. I've only been there once."

"Are you going back? Can I come with you?"

I shook my head. "I don't think you should come. I mean, my mom takes this very seriously and I think she'd be upset if, well, if you thought it was just a goofy thing to do."

She sat back in her seat. "I probably wouldn't really want to go, anyway. I'd be scared. I don't want to talk to dead people."

We got off the bus near Tobias Elementary School, where Paul's team's game was taking place.

"So, are you going home or coming with me to the game?" Roxy wanted to know.

I hesitated. There was no particular reason to go home, but I also had no real interest in basketball. Not that that had much to do with my decision.

"Nathan will be there," Roxy said in a singsong voice.

"Why do you think I care whether Nathan is there or not?" I sputtered.

"Oh, come on, Liz. You *so* have a crush on him. And you should—he's adorable!"

I opened my mouth to protest, but I didn't know what to say. Roxanne was no idiot, and this was her area of expertise. Okay, I probably did have a crush on him, but what was the point of dwelling on it? It wasn't going to happen. And I couldn't tell Roxanne why it wasn't going to happen.

"He's not *that* cute," I said as we walked toward the basketball court.

She laughed. "Well, he's not as cute as Paul."

"What? He's way cuter than Paul!"

It was already three thirty, and the game was more than half over. Thank goodness. I never understood what was so much fun about watching a bunch of sweaty guys run up and down a basketball court. Of course, I'd never watched Nathan play before either.

He played like a maniac, getting all up in the other team's faces and practically growling at them. He'd steal the ball and race downcourt like his pants were on fire, then leap into the air to make the shot. He didn't always hit the basket, but he hit it often enough. And talk about sweaty— water was pouring down his face, and his shirt was soaked through. I'd always found this kind of athletic showing-off pretty disgusting, but for some reason I didn't mind so much when it was Nathan.

There were a few other girls watching the game, but no other guys. Another thing I never liked: boys playing sports, girls applauding them from the sidelines. It seemed like when you were a kid, the mothers sat on the bleachers and applauded, and then when you got older, the girlfriends did. How come females always watched males and said *Go, you!* It kind of sucked. And yet, here I was sitting on a bench yelling for the Mustangs.

They won, thirty to twenty-one and all the sopping-wet guys slapped each other's backs afterward. Paul headed over to Roxanne, and Nathan trailed behind him.

"Eeuw," Roxy said. "Don't touch me—you're filthy!"

Paul held his shirt away from his skin. "Yeah, and I stink, too."

"Thanks for the warning." She took a step back from him.

Paul looped an arm around Nathan's neck. "Did you see this guy play? He's a madman out there!"

Nathan smiled sheepishly. "Sorry. I got caught up in it."

"Hey, don't apologize. You won the game for us, bro."

"You were *amazing,*" Roxanne assured him.

Now it was my turn to say something. "Yeah, you were really good." Inspired.

We glanced at each other and then looked away.

"I know," Paul said. "Nathan and I can go to my place and shower, then meet you guys at the lake in half an hour."

"Okay!" Roxanne said. I knew she was anxious to wear the new bikini she'd gotten this year.

Nathan's response wasn't so enthusiastic. "Um, I don't have a suit with me—"

"You can borrow one of mine," Paul said. "We're about the same size."

Of course Nathan didn't want to go to the lake, especially not with me. That was the scene of our last uncomfortable talk. I'd save him the trouble of coming up with another lame excuse.

"Oh, I can't go," I said. "But you guys should all go. I promised my dad that I'd . . ." What would I have promised my father? What? "That I'd help him make dinner tonight. He's teaching me to make pizza dough."

Roxanne stared at me, not buying it. "You'd rather make pizza dough with your father than come to the lake with us?"

"I *promised* him. Besides, Saturday night is sort of family night. You know, pizza and a movie."

Roxanne rolled her eyes. "Everywhere else on earth Saturday night is date night. Family night is for ten-year-olds."

"Well, not at my house," I said, already turning around and starting down the street. I didn't even look at Nathan.

"Can't you at least wait for me to walk with you?" Roxy said. I could tell she was appalled by my rapid escape.

"I'm late already," I yelled back, hoofing it away from them as fast as I could. "I'll talk to you later."

"Damn right you will!" she hollered after me.

Chapter Twelve

*L*et's see, how many people were mad at me simultaneously? Mom, Courtney, Roxanne . . . maybe Nathan? It might not have been a world record, but it was certainly my personal best.

Mom came back from church looking pleased, but she wouldn't tell me what had happened there. Humming quietly, she went out to her studio to trim some pots. She remained silent through dinner, which was the usual homemade pizza I'd mentioned to Roxanne—produced with minimal help from me—but the scene was hardly the contented family picture I'd painted for her.

We'd been wolfing down pizza in silence when I dared to ask Mom, "So, how was church today? Did Reverend Samuel do your reading?"

Mom glanced at me briefly, as if she'd forgotten I was

there, then took another doughy bite, obviously not intending to answer me. Sometimes I wondered why I kept trying. Mom and I were never going to be buddies. Why didn't I just give up?

Dad stopped scarfing salad and glared at her. "For God's sake, Christine, you're acting like a petulant child!"

She fixed him with a frosty look. "In what way?"

"You know *in what way*. Refusing to talk about what happened today. It's immature."

"Oh, I forgot, you're the expert on maturity." She picked the asparagus daintily off her slice and popped it in her mouth. "Liz would know what happened if she'd come with me. And I didn't think you wanted to know, since all my church friends are *nuts* and *crazies*."

Her smile seemed to infuriate Dad all the more. He dropped his fork and it clanked onto the table. "Forget about me. You're punishing your daughter just because she isn't embracing your new beliefs as wholeheartedly as you do. Would Bunny have done that to you?"

I was so shocked by Dad's attack, I gasped. Mom's smile crumpled and her eyes welled with tears immediately. "That is the cruelest thing you've ever said to me."

"Well, maybe it's time for some tough love around here," Dad grumbled.

Mom left the table then, throwing her pizza into the sink as if it were contaminated. As she raced upstairs, Dad and I looked at each other guiltily. I was glad he'd stood up for me, but I felt bad that it had hurt Mom so much. Didn't he know that she was very fragile right now? He should have backed off—I could live without knowing what had happened at the Spiritualist Church, and obviously I was going to.

Very little pizza was consumed that night.

But the next morning Mom was back in her studio when I got up, a Lucinda Williams CD turned up loud.

"Should I put the sign out?" I asked when I walked in. Once again I was the one making the peace offering.

She jumped a little when I spoke, but at least she didn't seem angry anymore. "Oh, Liz, I didn't hear you. Yes, okay, why don't you put the sign out." She gave me a small smile, which seemed to take a great effort, and I returned it.

I wasn't halfway down the lawn before the screen door banged open across the street and Courtney came running at me, her ponytail swinging wildly. She stopped a few feet away and planted her hands on her hips.

"Are you still mad at me?"

"I was never mad at you. I thought you were mad at me," I said.

She looked down at her worn-out sandals. "Well, I was for a while. But I told my mom about it and she said that teaching those kids was your job and everything. And Nathan said I was being a brat and I should be glad you let me go with you at all."

I put my hand on her head. "You weren't being a brat. You

just wanted to learn to play the piano—I understood that. I just couldn't give you lessons at the Romanows', that's all."

"Can you give me lessons *now*? At your house?"

"Well . . . I guess. Why not? Sure. Go tell somebody where you are and then—"

She was racing off already.

"Look before you cross the street, Courtney!"

She gave a cursory glance left and right, raced across the street, flung herself through the door, and in half a minute was back outside, running pell-mell across the street again. Her enthusiasm was as contagious as it was terrifying.

We spent an hour and a half at the piano; Courtney was a sponge, soaking up everything I said. She mastered scales easily, understood the concept of them, and was eager to move on to real songs. Fortunately, I still had some of my early sheet music stashed in a drawer—I hated to throw any of it away—so she picked her way through "Twinkle, Twinkle, Little Star" and several other nursery tunes before I called a halt.

"I'm hungry," I said. "Let's have lunch. Do you like turkey?"

"Do I have to? I *love* the piano. I want to play as good as you do!"

I promised her she could come over to practice in the mornings whenever she wanted, before I went to the Romanows'.

"And you'll teach me some more songs, too?"

"Yes, but you should learn these pieces first. Then I'll give you more."

Reluctantly she followed me into the kitchen. I made sandwiches and we took them out onto the front porch. As we sat there, looking across to Mrs. Crosby's house, Courtney seemed unusually quiet.

"You okay?" I asked her.

"Yeah." She was chewing a big bite slowly. "Last night . . . my mom got sick again. She threw up and stuff. This morning she didn't get out of bed."

Suddenly my turkey and cheese tasted like sawdust. How could I have forgotten for a moment how Courtney's life was soon going to change? Forever.

"I hate it when she gets sick," she said.

"I bet you do," I said, measuring every syllable I dared to say.

"Liz?"

"Hmm?"

"You think she's going to get well again, don't you? I mean, she's not always going to be sick, is she?"

Oh, God, why was she asking *me* these questions? I wasn't the person who could answer them—and now I was going to have to lie to her!

I stalled. "Well, Courtney, I don't know why your mom got sick in the first place—"

"But, I mean, people get well from stuff like this, don't they?"

What choice did I have? I took a deep breath. "Sure they do. Everybody gets sick and throws up once in a while. You've been sick like that, haven't you?"

She nodded happily. "Yeah. Last winter I was barfing for two days straight. It was gross. But I got well again."

"Right. And your mom will too. Probably." If we didn't change the subject, *I* was going to start barfing.

"I was kind of worried when she couldn't get up this morning. She looked sad when I went into her room."

I couldn't stand knowing what was ahead for Courtney, for all of them. Could. Not. Stand. It.

I jumped up. "I know, let's go down to the lake! Pete and Woody have been begging me all week. They said, 'Get Courtney to come and throw sticks for us again!'"

She smiled, but her enthusiasm had drained away. "Okay. I'll go get my suit." I watched her walk back to Crabby's house. She was walking so slowly that she actually paused at the street and looked both ways. I had the feeling she was looking for more than potential traffic down that road—it was as if she were peering into the distance for a glimpse of her future. Maybe she was thinking about her mother and beginning to wonder if she could believe the stories everyone was telling her.

As the week went on, I noticed that my parents had very little to say to each other, but at least that was better than the arguing. Mom went over to see Lily when I told her what

Courtney had said, and she reported that it seemed to be a temporary setback and that Lily was feeling better again. In fact, she was feeling so much better that Mom had asked her if she wanted to come with us to the Spiritualist Church the next Saturday. Lily had said she was curious and would join us.

"I assume you're coming with me," Mom said. "You did *promise.*"

"I *know*—I'm coming," I said. "But isn't it kind of weird for Lily to go? I mean, since she's . . . so sick?"

"I would think it would comfort her. Not that I think she's about to die, because I don't. But when you understand that your soul lives on after death and can communicate with the living . . . Well, I'm hoping it will help her to face whatever she has to face."

I hoped Mom was right and that Lily wouldn't get some weirdo reading from that faker Reverend Irene. Personally, I didn't think taking Lily to Singing Creek was the best idea, but I wasn't going to argue about it and make Mom mad again.

Friday morning Courtney came over for piano lessons as usual—she'd been at our house by nine o'clock every day that week—and then she tagged along to the Romanows' with me.

"I promise not to screw up the twins' piano lessons," she said.

"I gave them one yesterday," I told her. "None today."

She nodded, and I could tell she was preoccupied again. But Courtney could never hold anything inside for very long.

"Mom said that she and Nathan are going to church tomorrow with you and your mom."

"Nathan's going too?" That was a surprise.

Courtney nodded. "Mom said I can't come because it's kind of a strange church. And then Gramma said it would scare the bejesus out of me, whatever that is. How come you go to such a weird church?"

Just what I needed: more unanswerable questions. "It's sort of a church, but not a regular church. It's hard to explain," I said.

"And kids aren't allowed to go?"

"No, there usually aren't any kids there."

"I want to go," she said.

"Really, Court, you wouldn't enjoy it. It's boring," I lied.

"Then, why are you going?"

"I promised my mother I would. You know how sometimes you just have to do stuff you wish you didn't have to."

"Nathan *wants* to go. He said he wasn't going to let Mom go alone."

This kid heard everything. If they didn't hurry up and tell her the truth, she'd figure it out anyway. What were they waiting for?

It was a long afternoon. My time with Courtney was always filled with worry now—worry that she'd ask me a question I didn't want to answer, worry that her future was going to become her present much too soon, worry that she'd change.

When we got back to our street late that afternoon, Nathan was sitting on his grandmother's crooked porch swing, shucking corn into a paper bag.

"Grandma wants you inside, Courtney," he said. "She wants you to help her make a pie or something."

"Ooh, that's sounds fun! You want to help, Liz?" It killed me that this kid could even get excited about cooking with Crabby.

"Oh, I don't think so, Court. I should go home and practice the piano myself."

"Okay, see you later," she said, then turned back and gave me a hug before prancing off to bake pies.

"God, she's so crazy about you," Nathan said. "She talks about you *constantly*."

"She does? I'm crazy about her, too. She's great."

"When she's not a pain in the butt," Nathan said. He looked up at me. "Do you really have to go home right away?"

"Not this minute."

He handed me a stalk of corn from the pile next to him. "Then start shucking."

"Okay." I perched next to him on the swing. "I was hoping I'd get a chance to talk to you anyway."

"Yeah?" He looked at me, curious.

"Yeah. About Courtney."

"Oh," he said, turning away again.

"She's been asking me a lot of questions lately, about sickness, and whether I think your mother will get well."

"You didn't say anything, did you?"

"No, but I hate lying to her. And I think she suspects something anyway. When is your mother going to tell her?"

He ripped at his corn. "How the hell should I know? She never wants to discuss it. I'm starting to think she's *not* going to tell her."

"But she has to! If she just . . ." I lowered my voice to a whisper. "If she just suddenly dies, won't that be worse?"

Nathan stopped shucking. "Not for Mom, just for us."

I sat back in the swing. "I guess you're right. I didn't think of that."

"You know, some of this is your mother's fault," he said.

"*My* mother's fault?"

"Yeah. She keeps coming over here and talking about *miracles* and stuff. My mom never had any use for that kind of crap before. She was a realist—she always told me you have to take whatever life hands you and make the best you can of it. No miracles, no magic. That was, like, her motto. And now she wants to go to that crazy church with you guys to check if her soul is going to live on for eternity. I'm telling you, a month ago that would have made her laugh herself silly."

"A month ago my mother wouldn't have believed it either," I said.

"I wish she didn't believe it *now*," he said.

I pulled at my corn stalk. "Courtney said you were going too. If you think it's so dumb, why come with us?"

He stared at me, then looked away. "I don't know. Just to see, I guess. Just . . . just in case."

I nodded. "Yeah, that's why I go too."

We finished shucking the corn without saying much else. It wasn't uncomfortable, though. It was actually easier than I would have thought, sitting on Crabby's porch next to a guy I liked.

I finished two corn stalks and put them on the pile. "So, do you have to miss a basketball game to go tomorrow?" I asked as I got up to leave.

"Nope. The game is in the morning."

"Same place?"

"Yeah. You gonna come by and watch?"

I wrinkled my nose. "I don't know. I never liked sports that much."

He nodded.

"I like watching you, though," I said, then felt my face heat up. "I mean, you play really well."

"Paul was right: I play like a madman. I get so angry just sitting around here all week, but playing ball is a way to let it out."

"That's good, then. I'm glad you found out about the team."

"Yeah, me too. By the way, how was family night?"

"What?"

"You know, you had to go home and make pizza with your dad instead of going swimming at the lake."

"Oh, right. It was fun!" I said, but I knew the blush was rising up my neck.

"You're a terrible liar, you know. Why didn't you want to go to the lake with us? You like to go with Courtney." He was looking down at his corn, not me, which made it easier to answer him.

"Well, I just thought that, you know, you didn't want me to go. I mean, the other time we went . . . well, it wasn't so great."

He looked up at me from under a wave of hair. "That's not true. Actually, that was the best day I've had since I got here." He rolled up the bag of shuckings and walked it out to the garbage can.

I followed him. "It was? You could've fooled me."

He looked down at his hand, which was alternately making a fist and then relaxing. "I guess I'm good at fooling people. But any day that I forget about my mother dying for more than thirty seconds is a good one. Basketball helps. The lake helps. And I guess talking to . . . people . . . helps too."

What people? *Me?*

He punched my arm gently with that fist he'd been practicing, then picked up the half-dozen pieces of corn and walked into the house.

Chapter Thirteen

Well, if it isn't the hermit!" Roxanne called out as I approached the basketball court. "I called you twice this week and you never called back!"

"Sorry. I guess I've been busy."

"Too busy for a phone call?" She looked at Courtney, prancing along by my side. "Are you babysitting again?"

Courtney gave her the evil eye. "No, she isn't!"

I had to smile. "This is Courtney, Nathan's sister. We came to watch him play."

"*You* came to watch him play. I came because I was bored to death at home," Courtney corrected me.

Roxy grinned. "Ohh, Liz came to watch Nathan, did she?"

I ignored her as we took seats on the stone wall that ran along one side of the school playground. The game was already under way. "So, who's winning?" I asked.

"The Mustangs. Paul has already gotten two baskets," Roxy said proudly.

"How many has Nathan gotten?" Courtney asked.

Roxanne hesitated a second, then said, "Three."

Courtney nodded. "He's good at basketball. I'm going to be good at it too, when I'm taller."

During the game Courtney whooped and hollered for her brother and his teammates with endless energy. The more time I spent with Courtney, the more I liked her. And it seemed as if she liked herself, too. I hoped that strength would be enough to hold her together in the days to come.

The Mustangs won again. "Yeah, Nathan, you beat the crap out of them!" Courtney yelled as he and Paul walked toward us.

Nathan smiled at her. "If your grandmother heard you using that language . . ."

"Oh, like she never swears. And she doesn't just say 'crap,' she says—"

"Okay, okay, we get the idea," he said, putting his hand on her head.

He was breathing hard, but he looked more relaxed and happy than I'd ever seen him. I remembered what he'd said about basketball helping him to forget about his mother for a while.

He smiled at me, too. "You came."

"I came," I said, returning the smile.

"You guys rock!" Roxanne said, throwing her arms around Paul's waist. "So, are we going to the lake? Liz and I could go home and get some food and meet you there after you shower." She looked at me. "You can go this week, can't you?"

It was already after one o'clock. I had to go home and have lunch and then get ready to go to the church, but I didn't want to tell Roxanne that. I knew she'd have something obnoxious to say about it.

Of course, I didn't have to tell her. Courtney did. "Liz and Nathan are going to this church thing this afternoon, with our mothers. But I could go with you! Can I?"

"What?" Roxy stared back and forth between Nathan and me. "You aren't really going back to that crazy church again, are you? And making Nathan go?"

"I promised my mother I'd go today," I said. "And I'm not *making* Nathan go. His mother wanted to go, and—"

She turned her attention to Nathan. "Do you know about this church? They talk to dead people!"

"They *do*?" Courtney was all ears now. God, I really didn't want to get into this whole thing in front of her!

"That's not the only thing that happens there," I said. "They do healings, too—"

"Is that why Mom is going? So she can be healed?" Courtney asked, all excited.

I glanced at Nathan, whose mood was rapidly deteriorating.

"Is your mom sick?" Roxy asked. "I didn't know that."

We had to get out of there, fast. Fortunately, Nathan was on top of it.

"We should get going," he said to me. "I've got my grandmother's car, so . . . See you guys later." He grabbed Courtney's ponytail a little too aggressively, to lead her away.

"Ow! Stop it! I want to stay with Liz's friend!"

"You know what, Courtney?" Roxanne called after us. "Paul and I will come by and pick you up in half an hour and you can go to the lake with us if it's okay with your mom."

Under normal circumstances Roxanne would never have invited Courtney to the lake—the idea of having a nine-year-old along for the afternoon was not her idea of a fun date—but I knew her curiosity had been aroused by our conversation, and she probably figured she could get the gossip out of Courtney.

Paul didn't look too pleased by the plans, but Courtney was ecstatic. "Sure! I'll bring some food, too!"

Nathan didn't argue with her. Since Courtney didn't actually know what was going on with her mother, she wouldn't be able to tell Roxanne much. Still, Roxy might be able to put two and two together. We rode home in silence, except for Court who was singing her own song: "I'm going to the lake, to the lake, to the lake. I'm going to the lake!"

Courtney had already left by the time the rest of us piled into our car to head for Singing Creek. Mrs. Crosby was standing on the porch to let us know what she thought of our plans for the day.

"Craziest thing I ever heard of, you all trooping off to commune with the *spirits*. And meanwhile, you let your child go to the lake all by herself!"

"She's not all by herself, Mother," Lily said. "She's with Liz's friend Roxanne."

Crabby brushed that comment away. "I don't trust that Roxanne. She's too flighty. And I see she's got a boyfriend, so you can just bet she won't spend two minutes keeping an eye on Courtney."

"Courtney is a fine swimmer, Mom. You don't need to worry about her."

"I'm not worrying," Crabby said angrily, as if she'd been accused of a crime. "I just think somebody should be a little more responsible, is all."

The rest of us were in the car already; Lily slammed her door and sighed. "As usual she means me. *I'm* not responsible enough."

"That's silly," Mom said. "Roxanne is perfectly capable of—"

"That's not what she's really talking about. She probably doesn't even know it, but what she really means is, how could I dare to die and leave her with two children. That's what's really scaring the stuffing out of her." Lily leaned her bony shoulder against the car door and let her head rest against the window. "It's scaring me, too, believe me."

Nathan and I were in the backseat. Even though I didn't look over at him, I could feel the pressure building on his side of the car. After a silent minute or two, he blew.

"Well then, why *are* you leaving us with her? She's impossible! She doesn't even like us!"

Lily sighed. "She doesn't express her feelings well, Nathan. Or rather, she expresses them inappropriately. But she does like you. Or, at least, she loves you—you're family."

"But she's awful! We could stay with somebody on the Cape. Linda said we could stay with her, or I could stay with Michael's family, and Courtney could stay—"

"It was nice of Linda to offer—she was trying to help, but she's a single mother with three kids of her own. How could she afford to take in two more? And I don't want to split you and Courtney up. She's going to need you, Nathan. And you're going to need her, even if you don't think so. Your grandmother is your family."

"So she has to take us, even if she doesn't want to," Nathan muttered. "Some plan."

After that we all pretty much leaned against our own windows, thinking our own depressing thoughts, until Mom pulled into the parking area at Singing Creek.

"The water is down there," she said, pointing, as we climbed out of the car.

"I can hear it," Lily said, "but I'm kind of tired already. I think I should go in and sit down."

"Of course," Mom said. "You two can go have a look

if you want." She motioned to Nathan and me.

But Nathan didn't care about a creek singing, dancing, or playing the flute. As soon as our mothers disappeared inside the building, he leaned against the car and let his head drop into his hands. "Maybe this wasn't such a good idea," he said.

"Because your mom will get too tired, you mean?" I asked.

"Not just that." He looked at me with big sad eyes. "I know it sounds awful, but I don't want us to get our hopes up again. I mean, you think you've figured out how to deal with this bad thing that's happening, how you can get through it without completely losing your mind, and then suddenly something makes you feel a little bit hopeful. You start to think, *maybe*—to believe there could be a miracle. But there never is, and when the truth hits you again, it hurts twice as much as it did before."

I'd never seen anyone look so miserable. I hardly even realized I was doing it—my arms seemed to move by themselves, to surround Nathan and embrace him. He hugged me back and we stood there for a minute, each feeling the comforting warmth of the other person. I'd never had my arms around a boy before, or vice versa, but it didn't seem strange at all. It seemed right. I could have stood there all afternoon if Monica Winters hadn't shown up.

"Is that you, Liz Scattergood?" she yelled. "I don't think this is an appropriate place for that kind of behavior, do you?"

Nathan and I jumped apart, embarrassed, even though there was nothing to be embarrassed about.

When I turned to face her, Monica laughed. "I'm just kidding. I've done worse in my life," she said. "At least you're not in the backseat of the car! Is your mom inside already?"

What an idiot she was! I nodded and she went on inside, shaking her head at the memories of her own "inappropriateness."

"I guess we better go in," Nathan said.

"We don't have to if you don't want to," I said.

"No, I want to," he said, sighing. "You know, just in case."

By the time we got inside, Monica was sitting next to Mom, yakking at her and Lily. If she didn't put Lily off Spiritualism, nothing would. Was she telling them we were hugging in the parking lot, or could she manage to mind her own business for two seconds?

Nathan and I sat on the other side of the pew, he next to his mom and me on the end, as far from Monica as I could get. The healing part of the service started soon after. The old harp player was absent, but a youngish woman in an Indian-print dress played the piano, badly. Nathan wasn't interested in the healing stuff, but I told him it didn't take long and you couldn't have a reading without a healing, so he went up too.

Running Fox did my healing again. Monica got him too, but Mom, Lily, and Nathan all got Reverend Samuel. When they sat back down, Lily looked even paler than before. Nathan whispered something to her, and she shook her head.

"Is she okay?" I asked him.

"She says she's just tired. I don't know. This might be too much for her."

There were a few songs, and Reverend Irene gave a little speech about opening up your mind and heart so the spirit could come to you. Then she did a few readings, Monica's among them. Something about a chair that kept on rocking and the letter *F.* More of her rambling, which seemed ridiculous to me, but obviously it meant something to Monica—or, at least, she pretended it did. I looked over and saw Mom comforting her while tears ran down Monica's cheeks. *Please.* Nathan got Reverend Irene too, which was too bad. If anybody could make you think it was all garbage, it was her. But maybe that was all right since Nathan didn't really want to believe in Spiritualism, anyway.

With Nathan she got on a long-winded monologue about trains and about circling back and being late. I was surprised that Nathan seemed to be interested in it. She also told him there was a man standing behind him who had something to do with the trains. When she said that, Nathan sat up straight and I could tell he was resisting the impulse to turn around and look. She told him a lot of other unrelated stuff too, but it was the train stuff he seemed most interested in.

Reverend Samuel was up next, but he only did a few people, Mom among them. She liked him, so I knew she'd be pleased. His hands began to spin as they had before and his eyes went out of focus as he looked for what the rest of us couldn't see, but the reading didn't seem too informative to me. A lot of stuff about planting flowers—all the mediums had a lot to say about flowers and I wondered if gardening could really be such a big concern in the afterlife. Once again he got the letters *E* and *L*—he was sticking to that story. Then he said something about the color blue and an infinite body of water. "Maybe an ocean," Reverend Samuel said. Mom was nodding at this, but I couldn't imagine what she thought it meant.

Running Fox, aka Reverend Peter, came to the podium next. He seemed much calmer than the other two mediums. He flicked his white ponytail over his shoulder and closed his eyes for a minute, then opened them and stared straight at me.

"The girl in the yellow blouse," he said. "May I come to you?"

"Yes, you may," I answered.

He smiled at me. "You know who walks with you, don't you?"

I nodded, because I didn't know what else to do. If anyone was going to be reaching me here, it was likely to be Bunny, so I guessed I knew who he was talking about, or who I wanted him to be talking about. "She is here. She is happy for you. Her eyes are bright and her arms are open. She tells me you are strong, stronger than those around you. You can be of help to them, she says. Don't think you can't." I felt Mom and Monica staring down the pew at me, but I didn't look back. I liked Running Fox's low, soft voice and I was comfortable with him as a storyteller—someone who helped me think about Bunny in a happy way. But I hated that Mom thought he was proving something to me. Something that was impossible to prove.

"She holds a small animal as if she would like to give it to you. A cat, I think, or some other small, furry animal. She loves you very much." He smiled at me then, and I thanked him for the reading. I wondered if he'd known that my grandmother was named Bunny. Or was the "small, furry animal" just a coincidence? Mom reached across Lily and grabbed my hand and winked. I knew it was enough proof for her, and I wished it was enough for me, too. I wondered, if Bunny really was trying to communicate with me and I didn't believe it, wouldn't that hurt her feelings? I would hate for that to be true. Or maybe your feelings didn't *get* hurt after you died.

Finally, when almost everyone else was finished, Running Fox did Lily's reading. I think Nathan and I were holding our breath, and maybe Lily was too. After she told him he could come to her, he said, "There is a man who would like to welcome you. He says you may not remember him, but he remembers you." I glanced over at Lily and saw that she looked frightened. Nathan grabbed her hand.

"I see the letter *G,* or perhaps *C.* He has something to do with a hammer. Maybe carpentry or building something. He shows me a photograph. I can't see it clearly. Perhaps he means to say he was a photographer. There are shells, a beach, a cottage by the beach. He is happy for you."

And that was that. A few more songs, an invitation to coffee and doughnuts in the room downstairs, and we were done.

"Are you okay, Mom?" Nathan asked.

"I feel a little bit light-headed," Lily said. "All the excitement, I guess. And it's so hot in here."

He helped her up and she staggered a little as we walked downstairs.

"Wasn't that amazing?" Mom said once we were outside in the cooler air. She walked backward in front of us as we headed to the car, anxious to hear our impressions. "What did you think? I just adore Reverend Samuel, but Running Fox is very good too." She waved good-bye to Monica as the rest of us slid into the car. She couldn't stop talking.

"I thought your reading, Liz, was particularly astonishing, didn't you? That *Bunny* should be holding a *rabbit*! If that's not proof—"

"He said cat, not rabbit," I reminded her.

"'Or some other small, furry animal.' That's what he said. And you *are* strong. He was right about that, too—stronger than I am."

"Oh, a rabbit!" Lily said. "I hadn't made that connection, but of course you would."

"It was amazing, wasn't it?" Mom continued. "What did you think, Nathan? Did your reading hit on anything?"

"Not too much," he said. "Just the train stuff. That was a little spooky."

"Yes, that was strange," Lily agreed. "We didn't go to contact *him,* did we?" She tried for a laugh, but it came out as more of a groan.

"Him who? Did the trains mean something?" my nosy mother had to know.

"Nathan's father had a huge train set that he kept right in our living room," Lily explained. "He was a nut about that thing."

"He wouldn't even let me touch it, much less play with it," Nathan said. "So it didn't mean that much to me. It was *his* toy."

"Well, that may be true," Mom said, "but it was his way of identifying himself to you. Do you see that? He knew you'd remember the trains."

Nathan shrugged. "Maybe. But there were other things he could have said. We used to go fishing together and we built a little sailboat one time. Those are the *good* memories I have of him. Why would he choose the trains? I hated those damn things. And nothing else she told me made any sense at all."

Mom sighed. "Sometimes things make more sense later," she said, repeating the party line. "Unfortunately, you can't question the dead. You just have to take what they give you."

"I'd rather *not* take it, thank you," Nathan said, but not loud enough for the front seaters to hear him.

"So, Lily, what did you really think? Was your reading good?" Mom asked.

"Good? I don't know. I was little unnerved that there was a man waiting to *welcome me*. Welcome me where? Neither my father, Milton, nor my ex-husband, Bill, had a name beginning with G or C. And either way, I don't know that I want them standing at the Pearly Gates, *waiting*."

"It's all BS," Nathan said, sounding suddenly furious. "The initials he gave you were meaningless, the carpenter stuff, the photographs, all of it was stupid. There's nobody *waiting* for you. I think they just get lucky once in a while and then people believe everything they say!"

This was my suspicion too, at least sometimes it was. The rest of the time I wanted Bunny to keep talking to me.

"What about the cottage at the beach?" Mom said. "He got that right. You lived in Wellfleet all those years!"

"Not in a cottage on the beach, though!" Nathan said. "We could barely afford an apartment behind the grocery store."

"Well, Nathan, you know, the medium isn't *reading* the information. He has to glean it from what he feels and sees. It's not an exact science." Mom sounded offended.

Lily turned around in her seat to give Nathan a look. "It was really an interesting afternoon, Christine. Teenagers are always skeptical, but it's given me a lot to think about. Thank you so much for bringing us with you."

"Oh, anytime, Lily. We go every Saturday, don't we, Liz?"

Rather than promising my endless attendance at Singing Creek, I distracted her with a question. "When Reverend Samuel said that about the color blue and 'an infinite body of water,' you seemed to get what he meant, but I didn't. How does that have to do with Bunny?"

"Liz, you know blue was Bunny's favorite color . . ."

I did? Bunny liked any bright color.

"And the body of water was obviously Monticook Lake. She loved taking picnics there. Ever since I was a kid!"

"But Monticook isn't exactly 'infinite.' You can see across it."

She sighed at my ignorance. "You guys! You have to use your imagination! The messages don't always come across exactly right. It's sort of like a game of telephone where the middle people conveying the message can get it a little mixed up."

But if you used your imagination, you could make almost anything that was said seem true. How did that prove anything? I wanted to believe that Bunny had held out a rabbit to me, but Running Fox had only said "cat," and I couldn't quite make the leap.

Chapter Fourteen

We drove up to Mrs. Crosby's house seconds after she'd pulled her own car into the driveway. She and Courtney were just getting out, Court holding a big dripping ice cream cone, but one look at Crabby's face and we knew their trip had not been for pleasure alone. Her nostrils flared the moment she saw us, and she stomped over to deliver her news.

Nathan was still helping his mother out of the front seat when his grandmother started yelling. "I told you not to let her go to the lake with strangers, but no, you trust everybody! And you leave me here to deal with the consequences, old woman that I am!"

We all looked over at Courtney, who seemed to be in fine spirits and perfectly healthy. She made a face and said, "It wasn't that big a deal."

"That's not what you said half an hour ago when you had blood runnin' down your leg!" Crabby said.

"Blood!" Lily clutched the car door. "Courtney, come here. What happened?"

Courtney walked nearer, limping slightly, then turned around and showed us a bandage on the back of her leg, behind her knee. "A dog bit me is all. It was an accident."

"A dog bite is not an accident!" Mrs. Crosby continued to rant. "That Roxanne was not paying any attention to her, and she wandered off to play with some strange mongrel."

"Roxanne was sitting right there. I was throwing a stick for Yolanda, like I did for Pete and Woody," Courtney said, appealing to me.

"You can't be playin' with strange dogs, Courtney!" Crabby said. "It was probably a pit bull or one a those kinds. They're trained to attack!"

"Gramma, I *told* you, she was a beagle. She got scared when these boys came running past making barking noises. They scared her and she jumped up and bit me. She didn't mean to hurt me."

Lily kneeled down to look at the bandage. "Oh, sweetheart, I'm so sorry. Did it hurt?"

Courtney shrugged. "Not that much. I had to get a shot, though."

"A shot?"

"Of *course*. She had to get a tetanus shot! We're just comin' from the doctor's office now," Mrs. Crosby said.

"Fortunately, the owner of the dog was right there when it happened—some tourist, of course, but at least she had the good sense to come over here with Roxanne and that boy when they brought Courtney home. She *said* the dog had had all of its shots and was not normally a mean animal—"

"Yolanda isn't mean! I told you, she just got scared!" Courtney was getting aggravated.

"Well, it sounds as though everybody did the right thing in the situation," Mom said, trying to restore some calm. "Roxy brought Courtney home; the dog owner was responsible—"

"*I* was the one responsible!" Crabby insisted. "The child was in tears and you'd all run off to that church of the spirits—"

"But I'm fine now, Gramma," Courtney said, smiling her sweetest smile. "The pistachio-chocolate-chip ice cream really helped."

You could tell Crabby really wanted to smile back—her face got a funny, twitchy look, and it occurred to me that she'd probably forgotten *how* to smile, it had been so long.

"Well, thank God for that," Crabby said finally, allowing herself to run a hand over Courtney's messy hair. "If only ice cream could fix everything that easily."

"So the doctor said she'll be fine?" Lily wanted to know.

"He gave me a prescription for antibiotics, too, just in case. But he said she's okay. Not to worry."

Lily took a deep breath and a tear slid out of her eye.

"Thank you, Mom. Thank you for being here. . . ."

I know Crabby saw the tear, but she got all sharp again anyway. "What choice did I have, Lily? You were gone!"

By this time Lily was holding on to the door handle of the car in order to keep herself standing upright. Nathan grabbed her arm to help her inside.

"The service has made Lily very tired, I'm afraid," Mom told Mrs. Crosby. "She needs to rest."

"I'm not surprised," Crabby said, but at least she stopped complaining about everything.

Mom followed Lily and Nathan while Courtney and I lingered behind. Courtney was giving me a few licks of her cone when we heard them all yell. By the time we turned around, Lily was slipping to the porch floor.

Mom and Nathan picked her up, one on each side, and Crabby held open the door while they carried her inside and laid her on the couch. You could tell how little she weighed by how easily they lifted her—like a few armloads of fallen leaves.

"What happened?" Courtney said, running to catch up. "Mommy?"

"I think she fainted," Mom said. "She must be completely exhausted. Don't worry. Look, she's coming around already."

"Oh, God," Lily whispered. "Did I pass out?"

"Just for a second. You'll be fine," Mom said. "Are you chilly?"

"No, warm," she said, licking her lips. Her face had turned gray white.

"I'll get a cool cloth," Mrs. Crosby said. "Do you need the—"

"Yes, you better bring it," Lily said, her eyes closing again.

Mrs. Crosby brought the washcloth and an empty wastebasket, which she set on the floor near Lily's head. "Just in case," she said.

Nathan glared at his grandmother. "If you hadn't started screaming at her the minute we got out of the car, this might not have happened!" he said. "You have to make a federal case out of everything!"

Mrs. Crosby blinked at him but didn't yell back. She looked over at Courtney, whose ice cream was running down her hand and dripping on the carpet, but she didn't reprimand her, either. Instead she pulled a chair up to the couch and began to wipe Lily's face with the washcloth. Lily moaned.

Mom stood up then and pulled Nathan and me off to one side. "Why don't you two take Courtney and go across to our house? This is awfully frightening for her."

It was awfully frightening for *me*—I couldn't even imagine what Nathan and Courtney must be feeling. Nathan, as usual, looked furious, but Courtney's face held nothing but terror. I had the feeling that, even though she hadn't been told, some part of her knew.

Courtney didn't object to leaving. She ran ahead of Nathan and me into the house, dumped the remains of her cone into the sink, rinsed her hands, and headed for the piano.

"Listen to what I can play," she commanded. And we did. She banged her way through half a dozen easy tunes as though they were Wagner's operas, scowling as she concentrated on the notes.

At one point, when the music was particularly loud, I turned to Nathan. "Somebody has to talk to her soon. It's not fair."

"I know," he whispered back. "But we're all cowards."

By dinnertime Mom and Mrs. Crosby had gotten Lily upstairs into bed. She was feeling a little better and had fallen asleep. Mom invited the kids to stay for dinner, thinking Dad would be making his usual Saturday night pizzas, but we got a call from him saying he had work to do at the school and wouldn't be home until at least eight o'clock and we should order out. I was pretty sure this was because family night had deteriorated into family argument night since Mom started attending Spiritualist services.

We let Courtney pick where we'd order from, and she chose Chinese, although you could tell her heart wasn't really in it. She was trying to pretend everything was okay—like we all were—but she wasn't that good an actress.

None of us ate much. After dinner Mom took Courtney into her studio to let her play with the clay for a while. Nathan and I sat on the front porch steps and looked across the street to his grandmother's house.

"I'm starting to believe this is really happening," he said, staring at the porch light Mrs. Crosby had left on. "I mean, I've known it for months now—she had the chemo and the radiation and I knew they hadn't helped her. Still, I don't think I really believed it. But today . . . she looked . . ." He couldn't finish his sentence.

There was no sense in arguing that she'd really looked fine, so I just said, "I like your mom a lot. I like the way she is with you and Courtney. And maybe this is a dumb thing to say, but you can tell that she doesn't want to die. I mean, she doesn't want to leave her children. She loves you so much."

He frowned and let his gaze fall to his knees. "All mothers are that way, aren't they? Anyway, nobody wants to die before they get old."

"I don't know. I think some people, if they were that sick, they'd want to give up and get it over with." I was thinking of my mother, of course. If she had the choice to stay here with Dad and me or be with Bunny sooner, would she take the latter option?

Nathan sighed. "Sometimes I feel like giving up myself."

I grabbed his arm, horrified. "What do you mean?"

He turned to me and looked into my eyes. "I'm sorry—

I'm not trying to be dramatic. I wouldn't have the nerve to kill myself, anyway. It's just that there are days, like today, when I feel so *sick*. . . ." He put his hand on his stomach. "My guts are churning and my head hurts and my heart is pounding out of my chest. It's like I can feel her dying inside of me. I'd do anything to stop feeling this way."

Right then I would have done anything to *help* him stop feeling that way. I wanted to give him a transfusion of whatever I had within me that might help. An injection of hope, a heart transplant—whatever he needed.

So, of course I put my arms around him again. It seemed like too small a gesture, but it was the only one I knew how to make. Immediately he pulled me closer, his arms encircling me. In a minute or two we were kissing, very softly and uncertainly, as if kissing were something new we'd just invented. Even though I'd never kissed a boy before, it wasn't scary like I always thought it would be. Of course, I never imagined my first kiss would be with a boy whose mother lay dying across the street. It was a very strange thing; I felt remarkably happy, and at the same time terribly sad, as if the kiss had infected me with Nathan's sorrow. Or maybe, I thought, some of his pain had transferred to me, and now he wouldn't have to carry all of it by himself.

We stopped kissing when we heard Mom and Courtney coming. But we kept holding hands—to break the link entirely was too difficult.

"Gramma called. She wants us to come home,"

Courtney said, stepping out onto the porch with Mom behind her. "She says we've bothered the Scattergoods long enough today."

"You haven't bothered us one bit," Mom assured her. "You can come here any time you want to—both of you." Her eyes rested on my fingers entwined with Nathan's, but they didn't linger.

"Come over for your piano lesson tomorrow," I said to Court.

She nodded. "Your mom says she'll teach me how to make things with clay, too. And we can have a hat-making party for my birthday next month, just like your gramma had for your mom. So I guess I'll be pretty busy." I could tell she was trying to find her old enthusiastic self; she seemed stunned by her own indifference.

Mom leaned down and gave Courtney a hug. "We're going to keep you occupied this summer, don't you worry."

The jealousy hit me so quickly, I made a little noise of disgust, and pulled my hand away from Nathan's. I knew it was ridiculous to feel that way. I loved Courtney too, and I wanted to help protect her from everything she was going to have to face, but still. When was the last time my mother had given *me* a hug, or understood what *I* needed from her? Where was my "hat-making party"?

Nathan put his arm around his sister, the first time I'd seen him be tender toward her. Courtney seemed a little surprised too, but she accepted it.

"I'll talk to you tomorrow," he said to me.

"Okay." I was glad to hear there would be a tomorrow that we could make plans for. I wished I could kiss him one more time, but that wasn't going to happen while Mom was standing there.

We watched them walk across the street and into the gray house. The porch light went off.

"I'm glad to see you like Nathan," Mom said as she turned to go back into the house. "He'll need a good friend."

Obviously, she knew what everyone needed except me.

Chapter Fifteen

After Nathan and Courtney left, Mom went upstairs and I sat and played the piano for a while. I played two Mozart sonatas because they made me feel like the world had some order to it and wasn't just spinning out of control. Sitting there, I remembered something Bunny had said to me once, which seemed odd at the time. She said that she felt closest to God when she was playing the piano. Then she laughed and said, "Maybe music *is* my God!"

I asked her what she meant by that and she said we all had to find God inside ourselves, in the things we loved most. And she couldn't think of anything she loved more than playing the piano.

It didn't make much sense to me at the time, but now that I thought of it, it was no stranger than anybody else's ideas about God. Maybe the world would be a saner place if music were a religion. Or if art were a religion. Maybe Mom would be better off if she prayed to the clay in her studio or her finished pots and vases instead of expecting Reverend Samuel to make everything okay again.

When Dad still wasn't home by ten o'clock, I took my book and went up to bed. Mom had already been in the bathtub for half an hour by then. She said she was hoping the warm water would relax her after an "emotionally exhausting day," but I was starting to think she'd decided to drown herself instead.

I heard Dad's car chug up the driveway and then the water drain out of the tub. I tried to keep reading but really I was just waiting to see what would happen next. I heard Mom pad downstairs in her bare feet. The screen door slammed. They were talking but too softly for me to hear more than a hum, even though I'd left my door wide open. I assumed Mom was telling him about the service, the dog bite, Lily's collapse.

I finally decided the only way to hear anything was to just walk nonchalantly into the kitchen for a cup of tea. But I was no sooner outside my bedroom door than Dad started shouting.

"You mean you dragged that poor sick woman with you to that damn place? What is the matter with you, Christine? Have you lost your mind?"

Mom's voice became shrill too. "I wish you'd stop

accusing me of *dragging* people to Singing Creek, Jack. Lily *wanted* to come."

"It's one thing to take your own daughter, but that family is barely holding on over there. It isn't fair of you to try to foist your cuckoo ideas on them. You're taking advantage of the circumstances!" Dad said, sounding disgusted.

"I am not! I'm trying to help them!" Mom insisted.

"Oh, really? Did you help your friend? Did she feel much better after the service?" he said sarcastically.

"She's a sick woman. I think the service did help her, but it was a long day for her, and—"

"Christine, I don't know who you are anymore," Dad said, more quietly. I crept to the stair railing to make sure not to miss anything. Dad was pacing back and forth on the living room carpet.

"Don't be overdramatic, Jack."

"*I'm* overdramatic? Christine, you think you can talk to your dead mother!"

"I don't talk to her; I *communicate* with her. And if you are so closed-minded that you can't accept this, then I can't talk about it with you anymore." I could see Mom heading for the stairs and I ducked back inside my room, closing the door halfway so I could still hear.

"You're right," Dad said. "We can't talk anymore. Which makes me very unhappy. *Very* unhappy. I never thought I would say this, but I think we should take a break from each other. What you've just told me confirms the decision

I've been mulling over all day. All week, really."

"What are you talking about?" Mom asked him.

But I knew already what he was talking about. My jaw dropped open and tears welled in my eyes even before he answered her.

"I took a room at the Waverly Inn," he said. "I need to be alone for a while to think about things. And maybe you do too."

There was a long silence while the house reverberated with Dad's words. I quivered as though I were inside a bass drum.

Finally Mom said, quietly, "You're leaving me?"

Us, I wanted to shout. He's leaving *us*! And it's your fault!

"I feel like I don't know who you are anymore," he repeated. "I understand that you're grieving for Bunny, but why can't you turn to me for comfort instead of to that church?"

"I don't know what you're talking about," Mom said. "I'm the same person I always was."

"Well, then, I'm seeing a side of you I never saw before. And I don't know how to deal with it. I'm not saying this is forever—I just need to get away and think about things."

There was another silent moment and I wondered if they were glaring at each other. Then Mom said, "Fine. Leave." Her voice was flat and cold.

I was crying for real by that time and trembling like a cat in a cage.

"Do you want me to talk to Liz?" he asked.

"Oh, by all means, give her your stupid excuses," Mom said. "Although, now that she's smitten with the boy across the street, she may be less captivated by *your* charms."

I knew she'd meant for the remark to hurt Dad, but it stung me, too. She made me sound like a child, "smitten" with a boy and "captivated" by my father, as if my feelings were silly. As if Dad and Nathan were somehow deceiving me, which I knew they weren't. I'd been holding the edge of the door with both hands and, without thinking about it, I backed the door up and swung it shut as hard as I could so that the slam echoed down the stairs.

By the time Dad got up to my room, I was wild with anger.

"How can you leave us?" I screamed at him.

"Baby, I'm not leaving *you*," he said. He tried to hold me by my arms, but I slipped away.

"I'm not a baby! And you *are* leaving me! That's *just* what you're doing!"

"I need time to think, Liz. It's been very hard for me since your mother started . . . since Bunny died. I'll just be in Waverly. You can come and see me all the time. You can even stay there sometimes if you want." His eyes were pleading with me to understand him, but I couldn't.

"Stay in a hotel room? You obviously don't care what *I* want or you wouldn't leave to begin with," I said as I ping-ponged around the room, staying just out of reach of his hands, which wanted to pull me into an embrace. No way!

The funny thing is that I knew I was really angrier with Mom than with Dad. She was the one who didn't give a damn about me, and she was the one who was driving Dad away. Why wasn't I yelling at her instead of him? Maybe because I knew it would hurt him more, and right then I really wanted to hurt somebody.

I could tell by the look on his face I'd succeeded. "I know you're angry now," he said, "but please call me tomorrow or the next day. If you don't call me, I'll call you. I'm still your father. I'll always be your father."

When he walked out the door, I slammed it again. I was in love with the sound of the slamming door. It sounded the way I felt, like, *Damn you to hell!* and *I hate what you're doing to me!* and *Life sucks.*

Lily didn't get out of bed the next day, and it looked like my mother didn't intend to either. Nathan and Courtney were sitting on their front porch when I went outside midmorning. I had the feeling they were waiting for me. We were all in crappy moods and wanted to get away from our depressing homes, so we got our suits and headed for the lake. Mrs. Crosby filled a basket with food for us like she had the last time, but, for a change, she didn't harangue us with a bunch of rules. All she said to Courtney was, "Don't get that bandage wet" and "Don't play with any dogs you don't already know." Which, I guess, was her way of saying it was okay for Court to play with Pete and Woody.

As we trooped down to the lake, the dogs ran circles around Courtney, begging for her attention, and she brightened up a little bit. I could have kissed those smelly old hounds for adoring her so much.

Nathan was quiet and so was I. I couldn't decide whether or not to tell him about my dad leaving. He had so much else going on in his life right now, it made my problems seem small in comparison. But I wanted to talk to somebody about what was happening, and I knew Nathan would understand how I was feeling.

No sooner had we spread our towels on the sand than I heard the voice of the one person I had specifically decided *not* to talk to about my problems.

"Hey, you two!" Roxanne yelled as she ran toward us in her stunning red bikini. "I was hoping you'd be here today!"

Paul was behind her and he hailed us too, then said to Nathan, "How's your sister? We felt bad about her getting bitten by that dog."

Nathan pointed over to Courtney, who was already playing fetch with Woody and Pete. "She's fine. And still a dog lover."

"Thank God!" Roxanne said. "It happened so fast, and there was *way* too much blood for me to handle. Ugh. It reminded me why I don't babysit anymore."

"I thought you didn't babysit because you don't like kids," I said.

"Yeah, that too, but *bleeding* kids are the worst."

"Hey, Courtney's a nice kid," Paul said, smiling at Nathan. "I felt sorry for her."

Okay, Paul had just been elevated in my book from sweaty jock to actual human being. And I suddenly had the disloyal thought that he was currently a few pages ahead of Roxanne.

"So, I guess you athletic males are going to swim out to the float," Roxy said, giving Paul a meaningful look.

He rolled his eyes at her but said to Nathan, "I'm up for a swim—you coming?"

"Sure, why not?" Nathan said.

The two of them raced down the sand and were halfway across the roped-off swimming area in seconds.

Roxanne and I sat down on our towels, at which point she pounced on me. "Okay, I saw you. You can't deny it!"

"Deny *what*?"

"Deny that you were sitting on your front porch kissing Nathan last night. Paul and I were on our way to the movies and we passed your house and *there you were*! I couldn't believe it! How long has this been going on? And when were you going to tell me?"

Dammit. When you lived in such a small town, it was almost impossible to keep anything a secret, but I didn't even know what was going on with Nathan myself—I certainly wasn't ready to talk to Roxanne about it.

"There's nothing going on," I said. "We were sitting there and it just happened."

"So that was the first time?" she wanted to know.

"Yes, and for all I know, the last time."

She smacked my knee. "Don't be silly. If he kissed you once, he'll want to do it again."

"Actually, I think I kissed him," I said, sighing.

Roxanne's eyes widened. "No shit? You go, girl! When did you get so brave?"

"I'm not brave. I just . . ." I couldn't tell her everything that had happened before the kiss. She couldn't know about Lily. "I don't know. We'd been talking about things and . . . I just did it."

"Well, I think it's fabulous!" Roxanne declared. "And it's about time, too. Welcome to the world of *boys*!"

"I'm not entering the world of boys, Roxanne. Just the small island of Nathan. And maybe not even that."

"Girlfriend, I saw that kiss. You are definitely in his time zone. Definitely."

The boys had reached the float by then and waved to us on shore. I joined Roxy in waving back, then lay down on my towel and felt almost happy. So what if Roxanne was wearing a red bikini? I was in Nathan's time zone.

Roxanne and Paul had to leave by noon because Paul's family was having some kind of cookout and they had to go to it. As long as they were around, Nathan and I seemed to be able to push our troubles to the backs of our minds and laugh with them, but as soon as they were gone, reality rushed back. It was lunchtime by then, and Courtney joined us for peanut butter and raspberry jam sandwiches.

"You forgot to bring bones for Pete and Woody!" she reprimanded me.

"I know. Is there an extra sandwich?" I said.

"There are about eight sandwiches, I think," Nathan said, looking into the basket. "Our grandmother seems to think we're going to starve if she doesn't force-feed us."

"She just wants us to get happier," Courtney said. "And she doesn't know how else to do it, so she makes us a lot of food."

You had to wonder how this kid got so smart. "You can give the dogs a sandwich, then," I said. "They love peanut butter."

Courtney made each animal sit quietly while she doled out their goodies. She ate two sandwiches herself while Nathan and I struggled to get down one each. When she'd finished her sandwiches and her dog obedience training, she grabbed an apple and got to her feet, ready to begin throwing the stick again. She was tirelessly in love with canines.

Once Courtney was a little way down the beach, an uncomfortable silence surrounded Nathan and me. I knew it was because of the kissing. What do you say to someone after something like that happens? I felt like he'd seen me naked, and no matter how many clothes I put on he'd always think of me without them. Maybe Roxanne had been wrong—maybe Nathan didn't want me to be a part of his world.

But then his hand reached across the sand and enveloped mine. He smiled at me and my smile quivered back.

"Thanks for last night," he said. "It helped."

I knew I was blushing, but I tried my best to ignore the fact. "Did it? I'm glad," I said.

"You're the one good thing about moving here," he said. "I don't know how I'd be able to handle this alone."

I squeezed his hand. "I'm glad you're here too. I mean, I'm not glad about the reason you're here, but I'm glad I met you."

"Me too," he said.

We were quiet for a minute, and then I said, "Something happened at our house last night. After you left." I knew Nathan would understand how I felt. It seemed as if he listened more closely to me than anyone else ever had before.

"My dad came home late and started arguing with my mom about going to the Spiritualist Church. He hates the whole idea of it. He doesn't like any religious stuff, but this makes him especially crazy."

"He doesn't go to church at all?" Nathan asked.

I shook my head. "My mom has dragged him to holiday services at the Presbyterian church in Waverly once or twice, but he hates going. It's a long story, it has to do with his father."

"So, he doesn't believe in God?"

"I don't think so, not really."

"Do you?" he asked.

It was a question I wasn't expecting, one I'd been trying not to ask myself. "I don't know. I mean, I grew up thinking I did. I guess I want to believe. But sometimes when I listen to Dad, I think he's right, that the idea of God is something people use to define right and wrong, which would be okay, but then they use it against each other. Like all these wars where both groups think God is on their side. The whole God-likes-me-better idea doesn't make any sense. Dad says you can be a decent human being without believing in God, and I think he's right. What do you think?"

Nathan stared at the horizon. "I don't believe in God. I guess I used to, back when I believed in Santa Claus and the Easter Bunny. They're in the same category, as far as I'm concerned. Nice stories you tell children, but something no rational grown-up could believe. Even the people who believe in him or her can't agree on what they believe. Is he a benevolent old guy who sees every sick birdie, or is she an angry God looking to punish sinners? Crabby's always talking about 'the Lord' as if she's got some inside track to heaven, which is totally ridiculous. My mother doesn't believe in God, and she's the best person I know."

"You're right," I agreed. "If there is a God, you'd think he'd prefer your mother to your grandmother." We both understood what I wasn't saying—that he'd surely let Nathan's mother live.

"Yeah, it doesn't seem like anybody's calling the shots.

It's just the luck of the draw," he said, his gaze coming back to me.

"I think my mother would say God has a plan that we can't see. At least that's what she would have said before Bunny died."

"Now she thinks the plan is to spend eternity stalking through the vestibule of the Spiritualist Church," Nathan said grimly.

"She isn't crazy," I told him, pulling away a little bit. But he squeezed my hand.

"I know. I didn't mean that."

"Or, if she *is* crazy, so is everybody else who believes in things you can't prove."

He smiled. "We got sidetracked. You were telling me about your parents arguing last night."

"Yeah." I sighed. "My dad said that since Mom had started going to the Spiritualist Church, he didn't know who she was anymore. He couldn't talk to her. And then he announced that . . . that he was moving out." Suddenly there was a catch in my throat, and I had to clear it to continue. "He got himself a room at a hotel in Waverly," I said, staring at my unpolished toenails and willing myself not to cry.

Nathan dropped my hand and scooted across the sand to sit closer to me. He put his arm around my shoulders, which made me shudder. "I'm sorry, Liz. I'm really sorry."

"Thanks," I said, and then made the mistake of looking

into his face, into those deeply sad eyes. Before I knew it, there were tears streaming down my face, tears for me, and for my family, and for Nathan and Courtney, and the whole lousy world. My head fell onto Nathan's shoulder.

"I'm sorry," I said. "I know I'm being silly about this."

"No, you're not," he said.

"I know people's parents split up all the time, but I really love my dad and I never thought . . . I just never thought . . ."

"I know," he said. And I knew he did.

I tried to pull myself together before Courtney noticed what was going on, but I wasn't fast enough. She came running over to see what was the matter.

"What happened, Liz?" she said, squatting down next to me. She reminded me of her mother reacting to the dog bite.

"Nothing, Court," I said, struggling to brush away the tears and sit up straight.

"You wouldn't be crying if it was nothing," she said, wise as ever.

"Liz got stung by a bee," Nathan said. "A bee sting really hurts."

"Right," I said. "On my ankle." I pointed to a reddish spot, which was probably an old mosquito bite. I smiled at her as best I could, my eyes all puffy and red.

Courtney looked from one of us to the other, frowning. She was learning to spot a lie from a mile away.

Chapter Sixteen

By the time I got back from the lake, Mom was up and bustling around the kitchen, a room she rarely visited except to eat. She was pawing through the refrigerator, opening Tupperware lids, sniffing the contents, then tossing the whole containers into the trash.

"What are you doing?" I asked, slipping out of my sandy flip-flops at the door.

"Isn't it obvious? I'm trying to restore some order to this house." She sounded furious.

I peered into the full trash can and pulled out a plastic bowl. "This spaghetti isn't bad," I said. "We just had it two nights ago. We could reheat it for dinner."

"I'm making a stir-fry for dinner. With broccoli and snow peas." She lobbed another container into the garbage.

"Well, I can have it for lunch tomorrow, then."

"I'll make you something fresh for lunch." When, I wondered, was the last time she'd made my lunch?

Splat. A container missed its mark and broke open on the floor, splashing artichoke dip in all directions.

"Mom, stop it! You're making a huge mess!"

She turned around and glared at me, a half-eaten log of cheddar cheese in her hand. "It's your father who's made a big mess, not me. Now I have to clean it up all by myself!"

I knew she wasn't talking about leftovers anymore, but I said, "I'll help you, Mom. Don't worry."

"I'm not worried, Liz, I'm angry!" The cheese descended into the full basket and bounced off the top.

For some reason it pushed my buttons to watch that cheese, which was perfectly fine cheddar, hit the reject pile and then crash-land in the artichoke dip. I felt like she was throwing *me* into the trash, and I was suddenly furious with her. Didn't she ever think *she* might be wrong?

"Stop throwing everything away!" I yelled. "You're getting rid of stuff that's perfectly good!" I knelt down to retrieve the cheese.

"Don't raise your voice to me, Liz. I'm not the one who's caused the problems around here."

I couldn't let her get away with it. "Yes, you are! You knew Dad was upset about the Spiritualist Church, but you had to keep telling him about every detail of it, as if you were *trying* to annoy him. Couldn't you have just gone there and kept it to yourself?"

What was I doing? There was nothing I hated more than having Mom mad at me, and here I was telling her she was wrong—the one thing she would never admit to.

"So, you're on *his* side now, are you? I thought you understood about the church, I thought you believed in it." Her voice was as cold as her stare.

"I don't know what I believe," I said. "And I'm not on anybody's side, except my own!"

She shook her head. "If your grandmother could see your disloyalty, she would be ashamed of you."

That was really too much. "No, she wouldn't! Bunny loved me all the time—not just when I agreed with her."

Her face thawed out and drooped into long wrinkles. "I can't believe you'd say that to me, Elizabeth. Bringing Bunny into the argument when you know how much I—"

She wasn't getting out of it that easily. "You're the one who brought up Bunny! Besides, don't you think I miss her too? Why do you get to be the only one who's sad? I loved her as much as you did!"

"You did not!" she screamed, lobbing a bag of baby carrots in my direction. "You couldn't!"

That did it. My pent-up anger burst through the wall that had held it back for years. "I did too! You don't know everything, Mother! And you don't know me at all! You've never *tried* to know me. You're so good with Courtney, but you never had time to teach me to make pots, did you? I could *work* in your studio, make change when you needed help, but I could never *play* in it."

She shook her head. "That's ridiculous. You were never interested—"

"You were too selfish to notice if I was interested or not. The studio was the place you shared with Bunny, not me. And Bunny felt bad about it too. She said she'd spoiled you, and she was right!"

Her mouth dropped open in shock. For a minute we stood there glaring at each other, steaming mad. Mom finally broke the silence by slamming the refrigerator door. "Since you're such an expert on what's spoiled and what isn't, you can clean up this mess. I have better things to do with my time than argue with a child." She stepped over the slop on the floor and headed for her studio.

I knew she thought calling me a child was the worst insult she could come up with. She never liked being reminded that I was one, even when I was little. I think she thought she'd have a kid who would immediately grow up and become to her what she was to Bunny—a worshipper. Well, Bunny was *worth* worshipping.

I spent the next hour madly cleaning up the kitchen, repackaging food that was still edible, dumping the rest down the disposal, washing out Tupperware containers, and wondering if my mother had actually, finally, heard me. I mopped the floor and then started in on the fridge, thinking the whole time, *We'll never make it without Dad.*

· · ·

Nathan called the next morning.

"Are you going to your babysitting job today?" he asked.

"Actually, I'm not," I said. "I have a dentist appointment this morning, so Mrs. Romanow said I could skip today. Why?"

"Oh, I was hoping you could take Courtney with you. Mom's not doing very well and Courtney's pretty upset."

"Shoot. I can take her with me tomorrow."

"Okay. Maybe I'll take her along to my basketball practice."

"And when I get back from the dentist, I can give her a piano lesson."

"That would be good," he said.

"Is your mom . . . really bad?" I asked.

He sighed. "Hard to know. She's not good."

"Nathan . . ." I couldn't say it again. It wasn't really my business, anyway.

But he knew what I was thinking. "I *know*. Somebody has to talk to Courtney. I know it. . . . I just don't know how to do it. And it might be . . . too late for Mom to do it."

I swallowed past a lump in my throat. "Oh, God, Nathan. I hope not."

"Yeah, me too. How are things at your house?"

I sighed. How could I tell him that I'd yelled at my mother for cleaning out the refrigerator when his mother couldn't even get out of bed? "Not too bad," I lied. "It's a little strange not having Dad around." I didn't mention that

Mom and I were no longer speaking to each other.

"Yeah, I remember how that feels," he said. "Listen, I have to go. Courtney's coming downstairs. Talk to you later, okay?"

"Okay," I said, but he was already gone.

Mom drove me to the dentist in complete silence. In the waiting room she met a woman she knew and talked to her as if there were nothing whatsoever wrong with her screwed-up life. I got my teeth cleaned and checked, Mom had a friendly chat with the receptionist about booking another appointment in six months, and then we returned to our silent tomb of a car. The tomb of the unknown teenager. I knew she expected me to apologize to her, but I didn't intend to. I hadn't done anything wrong.

I couldn't wait to get back home and get away from her. But as we got near our house, I could tell something was wrong across the street. Mrs. Crosby's car was parked out in front and the rear door was hanging open. Her screen door was propped open too, and I could hear screaming coming from inside.

"Oh, my God," Mom whispered, pulling our car over in back of Mrs. Crosby's. In a second we were both running up the path into the house.

The scene inside was chaotic, and at first I couldn't figure out what had happened. Lily was lying on the couch, groaning, her nightgown hitched up around her hips, her knees pulled up to her chest. Mrs. Crosby was sitting next to her, holding her hand and weeping so hard that the front of her shirt was sopping wet. Courtney, of course, was the one screaming—and while she screamed, she beat her fists against Nathan who was backed against a wall, trying his best to hold her off and calm her down simultaneously.

"Stop it, Courtney," he said. "Let me talk to you. If you stop hitting me—Ow!" She'd landed a punch in his stomach.

"I hate you!" she screamed, then turned to see my mother and me walk in. "I hate you *all*! You're a bunch of liars!"

I got it then. Lily had obviously taken a turn for the worse and someone had finally told Courtney what was going on. I headed for Court while Mom went for Mrs. Crosby and Lily. I put a hand on the girl's arm, and she swung around and bashed me in the shoulder. She was a whirlwind of anger.

While she was focused on me, Nathan was able to get her from behind and pin her arms down against her sides. "Stop hitting people, Courtney," he said. So instead of hitting she lifted her leg and kicked it backward into Nathan's kneecap.

"Goddammit!" he said. "That really hurt, Courtney!"

"I *want* to hurt you! I hate you! You knew all along and you didn't tell me!" But the strength was rapidly flowing out of her tense little body, and she slumped to the floor, sobbing. "You all knew and you didn't tell me."

Meanwhile Mrs. Crosby told Mom that she'd been trying to get Lily to the car to take her to the hospital, but hadn't been able to manage it. She was afraid her daughter would die right there on the couch in front of her terrified children. So Mom called 911 and helped Mrs. Crosby find her purse and dry her eyes.

But they didn't stay dry long. As soon as Courtney stopped fighting, Nathan turned on his grandmother. "This is all your fault! You don't know how to do anything!"

For a minute Mrs. Crosby squared her shoulders and looked the way she always did, defensive and aggravated. "Nobody else was ever gonna tell the child. Lily couldn't do it, you couldn't do it. So I did it. It was time she knew."

"She's a little kid!" Nathan screamed. "Don't you have any sense? You just blurted it out the way you do all your commands: 'Your mother's dying, so go tell her good-bye now so you don't regret it for the rest of your life.' Are you even a human being? No wonder my mother left here and never came back!"

"She came back . . . when she needed me," Mrs. Crosby said, but then her composure split apart again and the tears fell. "I did the best I could, Nathan. No one else would do it! I did the best I could!"

Courtney was crying so hard she was choking. She let Nathan pick her up then, and he sat in a chair, holding her on his lap. I stood next to them and combed my fingers through her knotty hair. Had Crabby really said that? After all that waiting for the right moment and searching for the right way to tell her, *that* was how Courtney found out her mother was dying? Still, I had to wonder if her reaction would have been much different no matter how gently the news had been broken. There isn't really a good way to announce something so terrible, which is why Nathan and Lily never got around to telling her themselves.

In a few minutes the ambulance was out front. The EMTs brought a stretcher into the house and laid Lily in the middle of it. She groaned when they lifted her but relaxed a little once they moved her outside. She whispered "Thank you" as she stared up into the cloudless sky, but the EMTs were too busy to hear her.

Mrs. Crosby was much too distraught to drive, so we all piled into Mom's car to follow the ambulance to the hospital in Waverly. No one wanted to talk, so Mom turned the radio to a soft, classical station and we pretended to listen to it. Courtney was still crying, but in an exhausted way. She was in the middle of the backseat between me and Nathan, leaning against one of us for a while and then the other, as though she couldn't find a comfortable position.

Mom parked the car near the emergency entrance and we all climbed out. She pointed toward a group of large maple trees on the lawn in front of the hospital. "Why don't you guys go sit in the shade? They won't let you upstairs right now, anyway. It will take a while to get Lily checked in, but I'll come back as soon as I can."

Nathan nodded and took Courtney's hand, which she allowed now that the fight had gone out of her. But then she turned back to Mom.

"Will you tell me if she dies?" she asked, her voice shaky but clear.

Mom leaned down and hugged her. "I will tell you everything, Courtney. I promise. No one will lie to you again."

I don't know if Courtney believed that or not, but she walked away with us while Mom held Mrs. Crosby's arm and led her into the emergency room.

When we got to the shade trees, all three of us flopped down to the ground as if our legs couldn't take another step. We lay back in the grass and looked up through the leaves. It was a gorgeous summer day, the kind you look forward to all winter and then take for granted when it finally comes. It was not the kind of day you should find out your mother is dying.

We were all silent for a long time, but finally Nathan let out a deep sigh and said, "I'll never forgive her for this. She should never have told you like that."

Courtney sat up and stared at her brother. "Don't be crazy," she said. "I knew something bad was going on—at least Gramma finally told me the truth. Why do you hate her for that?"

"It was the *way* she told you," I said.

Courtney shrugged. "That's just how Gramma is."

"Courtney, it made you go berserk!" Nathan said.

Court lay back down in the grass. "*What* she said, not how she said it."

We lay there for an hour more in silence, Nathan's and my fingers laced with Courtney's, until Mom came back to drive us home.

Chapter Seventeen

Dad called me a few times that week, but Mom always answered the phone. She was more than happy to pass along my decision not to speak to him, but she didn't tell him that I wasn't saying much to her, either.

Mom went by the hospital during visiting hours as often as she could and sometimes drove Mrs. Crosby, too. On Tuesday, Lily was barely conscious and the hospital allowed Nathan and Courtney to go into her room. Nobody said it, but I wondered if they thought it might be the last time they'd see her alive. Nathan said that even when his mother was awake, she didn't seem to know they were there.

But then Wednesday morning Mrs. Crosby called to tell Mom that Lily seemed better. Since Lily and her family were the only topics Mom and I exchanged words about, she passed the news on to me.

Mrs. C also said that Courtney had been crying a lot at night and not sleeping well. I thought an afternoon at the Romanows' might be good for her, so I asked her to come with me that day. She'd shrugged noncommittally, then plodded along behind me so slowly I kept having to tell her to hurry up so we wouldn't be late.

Even Jake and Emma could tell Courtney was not her usual self.

"You aren't pushing good," Emma complained at the playground.

"My arms are tired," Courtney said, letting them swing listlessly at her sides. So we switched pushing duties for a while, until Jake complained, at which point I gave up on the swings and led them to the sandbox.

Jake had a castle almost finished when Emma banged her plastic shovel on it and collapsed the towers. While I was talking to Emma about being mean to her brother, Courtney laughed at Jake and called him a big baby. It wasn't like her to be mean to the twins, and they both stared at her unhappily.

At lunch Courtney acted more childish than either of the five-year-olds, smashing her sandwich until the tuna fish squirted out the sides, and spilling her lemonade all over the floor. When I asked her to clean up the mess she'd made, she pouted and complained again about being tired.

I felt sorry for her, but I didn't think it was a good idea to let her get away with being bratty.

"If you want to come with me again, Courtney, you'll have to clean up the mess," I said. "I'm not supposed to be babysitting for *you.*"

She rolled her eyes at my attempt at discipline.

"Yeah," Emma said, echoing me. "She's *our* babysitter, not yours." I knew it wouldn't be long before Emma ordered Courtney to go home again, so, hoping to avert trouble, I took the twins into the other room and read them a story.

I could hear Courtney banging things around in the kitchen. When I checked on her, she'd cleaned up the lemonade but left the floor swimming in soapy water. I knew she could do a better job than that—she was behaving badly on purpose—but I had no idea how to correct the situation. Finally I turned on the television, which Mrs. Romanow didn't like me to do, put on a Disney DVD, and told all three of them to sit there and watch it while I mopped the kitchen again. I didn't dare give the twins a piano lesson, although they wanted one—that would certainly end in disaster. Fortunately, the twins were happy with *Lady and the Tramp,* and Courtney conked out on the couch almost immediately.

She was still groggy when we left at five o'clock. On the walk home she asked, "Are you mad at me?"

I told her I wasn't.

"Would you be mad at me if my mother wasn't dying?"

It made my stomach hurt to hear her say that, but I didn't intend to lie to her again. "Yes," I admitted, "I probably would be. You weren't being very nice today."

"If I wasn't being very nice, you should be mad at me, even if my mother *is* dying."

I took her hand. "Do you *want* me to be mad at you?"

"Yes," she announced, almost proudly, but then took it back. "No, I don't really. Except you *should* be. I don't know."

She looked so forlorn I couldn't have been mad at her if I'd tried.

"It's not fair," she said, letting her shoes scrape the sidewalk as she slowed her pace.

"I know," I said.

"My father is already dead."

"Nathan told me."

"*Both* your parents shouldn't die when you're still a kid."

I squeezed her hand.

"Do you think . . . Do you think I did something wrong?"

"What do you mean?" I asked.

"I mean, like, is God mad at me or something? Or at Nathan?" She looked at me with eyes that were about to spill over again. "Or at Mom?"

"No! Oh, Courtney, no. That's not how God works." Listen to me, explaining how God worked, as if I knew, as if I had a clue what God was or why things happened the way they did. But I wanted her to understand that she wasn't to blame—that nobody was. "People don't die because somebody did something wrong or bad. They just get sick. It's not anybody's fault."

"But why would God let my mother die?"

How was I supposed to explain things I didn't understand myself? As far as I could see, nobody understood it. Religion gave you easy answers like, *It's God's will* or *She's in a better place now,* but who really knew if that was true? Yeah, the people at Singing Creek thought they knew. They thought they communicated with a spirit world that was so close to this world, they could see shapes and smell smoke and feel the breeze. And, really, that didn't seem any stranger than believing that people looked down on you from heavenly clouds or burned in the fires of hell, or even that people just disappeared one day and that was the end of that. Anything might be true, but I was starting to think a lot of what people said they believed was what they *wanted* to believe to make themselves feel better. And maybe I should have said *It's God's will* to Courtney, or told her about Singing Creek to try to calm her down, but there had already been too much lying. Now I wanted to be as truthful with her as I could.

She was crying, but she just kept on talking. "Is it because Mom doesn't believe in God? Gramma gets really mad at her when she says that."

I put my arm around her waist and pulled her close to me. "Court, I don't know that much about God. But I think, if there is a God, he—or she or it—doesn't get mad at people. Maybe God watches us and listens to our prayers, but can't really do that much to change most things. God wouldn't make a nice person like your mother sick just because she didn't believe in him. If he did, he isn't a God I'd want to believe in, anyway."

"But you *do* believe in God, don't you?" she asked, drying her face on her T-shirt.

Why was it so important to everyone that you have an answer to that question? Why did I have to decide right now if I believed in God or ghosts or talking waters? I was only fifteen. I couldn't even *vote* until I was eighteen!

"I don't know, Courtney. I'm still thinking about it." I smiled at her. "Can I get back to you later on that?"

She nodded. "Okay." We started walking again, and Courtney gave a deep sigh, then said, "I guess my mom will find out before we do."

On Thursday morning Courtney came over for a piano lesson, but her heart wasn't in it and she kept making mistakes. I asked if she wanted to come to the Romanows' with me again, but she said she'd rather stay home and read library books than "hang around with those babies again."

I played a few Scott Joplin rags to try to cheer myself up. Then, just before I left, Nathan called.

"I'm glad I caught you," he said. "You want to go to O'Henry's tonight for dinner? I really need to get away from my grandmother for a while. Away from this house . . . away from *everything.*"

"Sure. What time?" I was happy not to suffer through another dinner hour silently picking at my mother's awful attempts at cooking. And I was thrilled to have some time alone with Nathan—since Lily's hospitalization that had been scarce.

"Can you go early? Around five thirty? I have to have the car back in time to take *her* to the hospital."

I told him five thirty was fine, even though it meant racing back from the Romanows' on a hot, muggy afternoon, taking a two-minute shower, and trying to find something halfway decent to wear on a . . . whatever this was. Sort of a date. I guess I would have called it a date if Nathan's mother weren't so sick. Life seemed too serious right now for dating.

Mom wasn't home when I got there, so I left a note on the table for her: "Gone for dinner with Nathan. Back by 7:00." Nathan backed the car out of the driveway the minute I walked outside—he wasn't wasting any time getting away. As I climbed in on the passenger side, Crabby came running out the porch door.

"You better take an umbrella!" she shouted as she waved a big black stick at the car.

Nathan rolled down his window. "That's okay. I don't need it."

"Take it. Weatherman says a storm's headed this way." She tried to stick the thing inside, but Nathan pushed it back out. I would have just thrown it in the backseat to satisfy her, but I guess he didn't want *anything* from his grandmother.

"I'm not allergic to rain," he said, trying to get the window back up.

"You get wet and sit in that air-conditioning at the restaurant, you'll be the next one sick," she insisted.

Nathan turned to stare at her. "I don't want your stupid umbrella," he said, enunciating each word carefully. "Do you get that?"

Crabby stepped away from the car as if he'd hit her. "Fine," she said, her eyes narrowing to slits. "Get sick, then. See if I care." She took her umbrella and marched back into the house, letting the screen door bang behind her.

The scene put Nathan in a dark mood, or maybe he'd been in one already. Who could tell? I couldn't seem to find a topic of conversation that interested him, and after a few attempts I stopped trying.

It started to rain just as we got onto the highway. At first Nathan didn't turn on the windshield wipers, and I wondered if he was going to pretend it wasn't raining. But the storm got worse and he had no choice. By the time we turned into the parking lot at O'Henry's, it was pouring so hard you couldn't see the building even though we were only ten yards from it. Ten soaking-wet yards.

Nathan turned off the ignition, but neither of us moved. After about thirty long seconds I said, "Maybe it'll let up."

Nathan smacked the steering wheel so hard it cracked— or else that was his hand. "Dammit!" he exploded. "Now I'm going to have to listen to how *right* she was. She always has to be right! I *hate* her!"

"I know," I said.

"I can't live with her! I *can't*!" When he turned to look at me, I saw that black circles had formed beneath his eyes, as though they'd been punched deep into his head.

"It's okay," I said, reaching out to touch his arm. "We'll figure something out."

He jerked away from me. "How? There's nothing to figure out. It's all too screwed up." He turned away from me, his shoulders hunched protectively around his neck.

I don't know why I did it—I certainly didn't think it through or anything—but the next minute I'd thrown open my door. "Get out!" I yelled to Nathan over the drumming of the rain.

"I'm not hungry anymore," he said, resting his head on the steering wheel.

"Get out anyway!" I commanded. Then I got out and just stood there next to the car, letting the rain pelt me. It was the long cool shower I hadn't had enough time for earlier. I put my head back and let the rain slick my hair against my head. I closed my eyes and opened my mouth so the water poured straight inside me. *God-rain,* if Dad was right.

I heard the other car door slam, and then Nathan was outside too. He ran around the car and yelled at me over the pouring, pounding noise. "What are you doing?" His hair was already plastered to his forehead and his clothes were soaked.

"Enjoying the rain!" I yelled back. I slipped out of my sandals and the wet blacktop felt cool and scratchy on the bottoms of my feet. "Take your shoes off!"

"But—"

"Just do it!" I ran across the empty lot and jumped into the biggest puddle I could find.

Pretty soon we were chasing each other around the lot, barefooted, laughing like lunatics, kicking puddle water as high as we could, getting soaked to the skin. We ran until we were out of breath, and then we leaned against the car and took big drinks of the storm. I'd had my eyes closed for a minute, and when I opened them again, Nathan was staring at me.

"Thanks, Liz."

"Don't thank me," I said, laughing. "I didn't make it rain."

But Nathan wasn't laughing. He leaned in and kissed me—harder and longer than he had the last time. His arms went around my back and mine reached up to his neck. Wow. I never knew drowning yourself in rainwater could be that romantic. I don't know how long we stood there kissing, but finally we realized the storm was letting up.

We broke apart then, but Nathan kept holding my hand. "If it wasn't for you, Liz . . . I don't know . . . I couldn't stand it. I couldn't stand any of it. You're the one good thing in my life."

I didn't know what to say, so I kissed him again. The rain was ending, but I wanted to stay under the shower of Nathan's admiration forever.

At some point the air had turned cool and we started to shiver. Nathan ran into O'Henry's to get us each a take-out chicken basket while I got an old blanket from the trunk and spread it across the front seat. When he got back, we turned the car's heater on, but, like the rest of that antique, it didn't work very well.

"Let's go back to my house," I said. "We can take hot showers and put your clothes in the drier. By the time we eat they'll be dry, and Crabby won't even suspect."

"Except for the fact that her car is parked in your driveway," Nathan said.

"Maybe she won't notice."

"She notices everything. But, you know what? I don't care anymore." He smiled a high-wattage smile that heated me up better than any old shower could.

Mom still wasn't home when we got back. Nathan took the first shower so his clothes would have more time to dry. I gave him an old pair of Dad's jeans and a T-shirt he'd left behind. It made me feel weird to see Dad's clothes again, and weirder still to see them on Nathan. While I showered,

Nathan got out plates and silverware, microwaved the chicken, and made us mugs of tea.

We'd just pulled our chairs up to the table when Mom's car came screeching up the driveway. She must have seen us through the kitchen window; she came in yelling.

"Where in the hell have you been?" Her glare blazed into my face.

"I left you a note—," I said, pointing to it on the refrigerator.

"What good does a note do me when I'm not home! I've been calling and calling and nobody answered! I couldn't imagine what had happened to you!"

It seemed really odd that she was losing it like this in front of Nathan. Usually she tried to make everybody else think she was a reasonable human being.

"Well, you didn't even leave me a *note*," I said, defending myself. "I didn't know where you were either."

"*I* am not a child, Liz. I don't have to account to you for my actions."

Which really made me mad. I'm a very responsible person, and I hadn't done anything wrong. Why was she so out of control over this?

"What is my crime here?" I asked her. "All I did was go out for dinner with Nathan. We got caught in the rain, and—"

"Nathan?" Mom looked startled and turned for the first time to the guest at our dinner table. "Oh, goodness. I didn't realize—I thought you were—I'm *sorry,* Nathan!"

Sorry, *Nathan*? It was me she'd been screaming at. And then suddenly I realized what was going on. Mom had seen us through the window and thought that Nathan, with his wet, slicked-back hair and Dad's old T-shirt, *was* Dad. She'd assumed I was breaking bread with the enemy. That was the problem.

Her tone of voice became sweeter, and she took off her raincoat. "I don't mean to sound like a shrew. I was just worried. And I was hoping you'd be able to make dinner tonight, Liz. I've had a long day."

Nathan spoke up then. "You can have some of our chicken baskets. They always put too much in them, anyway."

I got up to get her a plate. "Yeah, we'll share."

Mom grimaced. "All that grease. No thanks. You guys enjoy it. I'll just have some cottage cheese and a few grapes."

Which was the dinner she preferred, anyway. The thing about wanting me to cook for her was a lie. She wanted me to feel guilty and wanted Nathan to feel sorry for her. I slammed the extra plate back into the cupboard.

"Where were you?" I asked her as she assembled her carb-free, grease-free, daughter-free meal.

"I was in Waverly at Bunny's gallery. With a Realtor."

I was shocked. Since Bunny had died, the gallery had been locked up tight and all the upcoming shows had been canceled. Mom hadn't been able to make herself go near the place. "A Realtor? You aren't going to sell it, are you?"

She sighed. "Well, I can't afford to let it just sit there empty. Taxes are high on a downtown location like that."

I couldn't imagine the space ever being anything but Bunny's gallery. Closing the gallery for good would be like losing her again. "Maybe somebody else could run the gallery," I said. And then the obvious answer hit me. "*You* could, couldn't you?"

"Me? I don't know the first thing about running a gallery. It's a full time job, Liz. I'm a potter."

"But Bunny didn't know how either until she tried. You could do it." If I'd been a few years older, I would have offered to do it myself.

Mom was quiet for a minute as she arranged her skimpy dinner on a plate. Then she said quietly, "I know Bunny always hoped I'd take over the gallery someday. But not this soon. I always imagined she'd be there with me, showing me what to do. And besides, it makes me sad to walk through it. I keep thinking she's just around the corner, any minute she'll come out of her office with something to show me, some new artist she's just discovered. Just walking through with the Realtor was almost too much to bear."

"But you *can't* sell it," I insisted, though I knew better than to take that tack with Mom. "Bunny wouldn't have wanted you to!"

Mom turned her back on me and said, "Liz, I know you think you understand the ins and outs of your grandmother's mind better than I do, but in this case I'm quite capable of making my own decision about what to do with my life."

She collected her minimalist meal and wiggled her fingers at Nathan. "I'll eat upstairs with a good book and leave you two alone," she said, the crazy lady of ten minutes ago hidden beneath a plastic smile.

Nathan and I chewed our chicken in silence for a few minutes. Then he said, "I've never seen that side of your mother before."

I nodded. "She tries to keep the loony bird locked up, but it escapes from time to time."

He reached across the table and held my hand. "Sorry," he said.

I smiled. "Aren't we all?"

When we finished eating, Nathan had to get back to take Crabby to the hospital. We kissed again, and he climbed into the old heap and chugged it across the street.

As soon as he was gone, I dialed Dad's cell phone.

When he answered, I started to cry. It was hearing his voice again and realizing how much I'd missed it.

"Shh," he whispered. "It's okay, Lizzie. I'm here."

Chapter Eighteen

F riday morning Lily died.

Mrs. Crosby called Mom from the hospital, where she and both kids had been since six A.M. There had been a crisis overnight, and a nurse had called them very early. They'd gotten there in time to kiss Lily good-bye, but Courtney had held on to her mother so tightly that it had taken Nathan and a male nurse together to pull her off. Then Nathan held his sobbing sister in the hallway until it was all over.

Mom told me as soon as I came downstairs. She was still in her robe and had been crying. And even though we were barely speaking to each other, she put her arms around me. For a terrible second I felt almost happy, but then I remembered why she was hugging me—because someone else's mother was dead.

"I really thought it might not happen," Mom said, pulling away from me and wiping her eyes on the sleeve of her robe. "I convinced myself she might get well."

I wanted to say, *You can convince yourself of anything,* but I didn't. Instead I said, "She was lucky you were here to help out the past few weeks."

She smiled sadly. "I was lucky I got to be with her again. I'd forgotten how much I liked Lily."

I looked out the window toward Mrs. Crosby's house. "God, I feel so bad for Nathan and Courtney, losing their mother."

Mom stood at the window next to me and sighed. "Just like me," she said.

What? My anger sprang to life again. It was all I could do to not scream at her, *You're not like them at all! They're children!* But I wrestled the words back inside. What good would it do to argue with her? Especially now, I didn't want to push her any farther away from me than she already was.

In a strange way Lily's death was harder for me than Bunny's. Not just because Bunny was older—I'd never thought of her as old, and I certainly wasn't prepared for her to die. But when Bunny died, I was in the middle of it. I was crying for my *own* loss, for the changes it made in *my* life. And I didn't really care what anybody else was feeling. I hardly even noticed anyone else.

But with Lily's death it was different. I didn't know her very well, but I felt that I knew her children as well as I'd ever known anyone, and I guess I loved them both. Part of what made Lily's death so terrible was knowing the pain it was causing Nathan and Courtney—and knowing there was nothing I could do to make it go away. It reminded me of all the people who'd called and come by the day Bunny died, begging to help, to be allowed to do *something* for us, even though there wasn't really much they could do. I realized now how hard it had been for them to be sad themselves and sad for us too, and to feel so helpless.

Mrs. Crosby was on her way back to the house. Mom had offered to go with her to make the funeral arrangements, so she went upstairs to get dressed. She thought I ought to stay with Nathan and Courtney while she and Crabby were at the funeral home. It sounded like the right thing to do, but I was scared. What would I say? How could I comfort them when I knew there was no real comfort for something so terrible?

I sat by the window and waited for Mrs. Crosby's car to drive up. When it did, I was surprised to see that she was driving it herself and Nathan and Courtney were in the backseat together. They looked bedraggled and exhausted when they climbed out. Courtney took her grandmother's hand to walk up the porch stairs, and it was hard to tell who was helping whom.

"Let's go on over," Mom said, coming up behind me, throwing her car keys in her purse.

"Right now? Shouldn't we give them a few minutes?"

"Lizzie, it won't be any easier in five minutes. We might as well go over and see what we can do to help."

"At least you can drive Mrs. Crosby around and help her with the funeral stuff, but what can I do? Nothing. Not a thing."

Mom nodded. "I know it seems that way. But you can be there with them. They'll appreciate it."

I was not convinced, but I followed Mom across the street anyway. My heart was absolutely banging when we knocked on the screen door and walked inside.

The three of them were sitting slumped on the furniture, Mrs. Crosby in an overstuffed chair and the kids on the couch. They looked like they'd just run ten miles.

"Don't get up, Eileen," Mom said. For a minute I couldn't figure out who she was talking to, but when she went over and put her hands on Mrs. C's shoulders, it came to me. Of course, Eileen was Mrs. Crosby's first name. I'd never thought of her as even *having* a first name. It made her seem, I don't know, smaller. Nicer. Sadder. If that makes any sense.

"We just wanted you to know we're available to help you do whatever needs to be done." Mom put her purse on a table and knelt down at Courtney's side.

"I bet you didn't have breakfast, did you? Would you like me to make you some scrambled eggs?"

Courtney shook her head and stared at Mom as if she'd never laid eyes on her before.

Mrs. Crosby roused herself a little. "Honey," she said to Courtney. "You should try to eat a little something. Maybe just a bowl of cereal."

"I'm not hungry," she said, and immediately began to cry again. I'd been standing in the doorway, embarrassed by the scene in front of me, but seeing Court cry like that, her sobs pouring out the grief and confusion inside her, loosened me up. I went over and sat next to her on the couch and put my arms around her.

"It's okay, Courtney," I said, even though we all knew it was anything *but* okay. She sobbed so hard the front of my T-shirt was soaked in two minutes.

"Why don't I make a pot of coffee?" Mom asked.

Mrs. C was staring at her granddaughter, but she said, "Yes, thank you. That would be good. The coffee is in the right-hand cupboard." To see Crabby now, all shrunken into herself and almost polite, you'd never guess she was a dog-hating, kid-cursing lunatic.

I looked across Courtney and met Nathan's eyes. I'd been dreading seeing his tears, but his eyes were the same sunken holes they'd been the night before, not red or puffy or wet. He looked miserable, of course, but more than that I couldn't read. He let his gaze slip away from mine and began to study his fingers as if they were a great mystery.

Nathan and his grandmother each eventually drank a cup of coffee, and Mom got Court to eat a few spoonfuls of cereal. Mrs. Crosby changed her clothes and combed her hair. Then she and Mom left for the funeral parlor, taking along a dress for Lily, the pretty flowered one she'd worn to my recital the night I'd met her. Which seemed like a hundred years ago.

"Courtney ought to take a nap," Mrs. Crosby said as they were leaving. "We were up at dawn this morning."

Nathan nodded, but he was looking at the dress in his grandmother's arms, and I wasn't sure he'd even heard what she said.

"Court, do you want me to go up to your room with you? I could read you a story and maybe you'd fall asleep for a little while."

Now that she wasn't crying anymore, she looked too worn-out to move. But she sighed deeply and got to her feet. "Yeah, I'm tired," she said. "Will you read me the next chapter of *Anne of Green Gables*?"

I said I would, then smiled weakly at Nathan. "Maybe you should nap too."

"No chance," he said, shaking his head. But he closed his eyes and let his head fall back against the couch cushion.

Upstairs, Courtney slipped out of her shorts and pulled her nightgown over her head. She snuggled in next to me and said, "I feel like I'm having a bad dream, Liz."

I didn't know what to say, so I kissed her on the forehead and ran my fingers through her tangled hair. She fell asleep before I'd read two pages. I arranged the sheet over her and crept back downstairs.

"That was fast," Nathan said, his eyes still closed.

"She was really exhausted," I said. "Aren't you?"

He nodded. "But I'll never sleep. I feel like I'll never sleep again."

I didn't know what to do. He seemed almost like somebody I didn't know. Not at all the same person I'd been kissing in the rain just the night before. I sat on the couch, but not too close. I felt as if there were one of those electric fences around him and if I tried to break through it, we might both be electrocuted.

We sat in silence for at least ten minutes, maybe more. Then Nathan said, "What am I supposed to do now?" He wasn't looking at me and I didn't think he really expected an answer from me, but I tried to find one anyway.

"I don't know," I said. "Help Courtney, for one thing."

He shook his head. "Courtney has her *gramma* to help her."

"But you're her brother. She needs—"

"I can't help her," he said, interrupting me. "I can't even help myself."

We were silent another minute, then suddenly Nathan perked up a little and said, "Actually, I was thinking about getting her one of those dolls she wants—you know, the one she told you about."

It took me a few seconds to figure out what he meant. "You mean a Sweetheart doll?"

"Yeah, that's it. Maybe that would help her get through this better."

"Nathan, they cost a fortune. And, anyway, I don't think a doll—"

"Like, how much are they?" he wanted to know.

"I don't know, seventy-five or eighty dollars, I think. A lot!"

He nodded. "Is there any way—Do you think you could . . . maybe . . . lend me the money? I know it's your traveling money, but I promise I'll get a job and pay you back as soon as I can."

I was pretty sure an expensive doll was not going to be the solution to Courtney's misery, but I figured Nathan wanted to do *something* for his sister and he didn't know what else to do. It's not as if I had a better idea of how to help her, and I wasn't going to be using my traveling money for a while, anyway. I went home and got the money while Court was still sleeping.

"Here's a hundred," I said, pressing the bills into Nathan's hand. "Maybe you can get the doll an extra outfit, too."

"Thanks, Liz." He stuck the money in his wallet. "I appreciate it, I really do."

"No big deal. I'm glad I can give it to you."

"Lend," he said.

"Whatever." I sat next to him on the couch, waiting for his arm to go around my back, waiting for my thank-you kiss. But Nathan sat motionless.

After a few minutes he closed his eyes again and rested his head against the arm of the couch.

"Maybe I could sleep a little, after all," he said.

On Saturday morning Mom and I took a quick trip to the Waverly mall to return the awful blouse and get a new one for me to wear to the wake. It wasn't the mother-daughter shopping trip I'd looked forward to, but we did find a pretty silk blouse that Mom had to admit looked better on me than the one she'd chosen.

"I wish you could come with me this afternoon," Mom said as we drove home. I still couldn't believe she was going to Singing Creek instead of spending the afternoon with us at the wake. Was she going to go there every Saturday for the rest of her life, no matter what?

"Mrs. Crosby asked me to stay with Courtney at the wake. And I want to do that, anyway."

"I know. But it's possible . . . I mean, Lily's spirit might be very close right now. She's just passed over. She might want to make contact. Maybe Nathan should—"

"Mom, don't even *ask* Nathan!" I yelled at her. "He'll think you're crazy. Besides, he wants to be at his mother's wake!"

"Don't get so upset, Liz," she said. "It sounds as if *you* think I'm crazy."

I didn't say anything.

"*Do* you?" she demanded.

"No, I don't," I finally said. "But I think you're obsessed with Spiritualism right now. I mean, there's nothing wrong with it—and maybe you really *can* communicate with people who've passed over—but not everybody believes this stuff. And you act like anybody who *doesn't* believe it is crazy!"

"That's not true, Liz. I know it's a difficult concept for some people, like your father." It was the first time she'd mentioned Dad to me since the day she'd purged the refrigerator of his leftovers, and I figured it was as good a time as any to try to get some information.

"Have you talked to Dad? Is he coming back home?"

"We've spoken, yes. I called him this morning to tell him about Lily. He said he talked to you last night, that you were upset."

"I want him to come home," I said.

"I know you do." Her eyes never left the road.

"Don't *you*? It's stupid that our family is breaking up just because you're going to Singing Creek. If you just didn't talk about it so much, maybe—"

"Oh, Liz, it's not just because of Singing Creek." She swung the car into the driveway and braked hard. "Your father expected me to cry for a few days and then forget all about Bunny, get over it. Just pick myself up and go on as though the most terrible thing hadn't happened to me. Well, I can't do that."

"I don't think Dad expected—"

"He wasn't close to his own parents and he just never understood my bond with Bunny, how *connected* a mother and daughter can be."

The words that had lain dormant my entire life finally flew out of my mouth. "Well, I never understood it either! You always talk about this magical mother-daughter relationship you had with Bunny, but you never tried to be connected to *me* that way! I'm *your* daughter. Where's *that* bond?"

I was glad to see the shocked look on her face. Her voice stuttered. "Well—of course, L-Liz. Of course we have a—a bond."

But I was suddenly furious with her again, and I wasn't going to let her get away with that lie.

"Bullshit!" I yelled. "You only liked being the daughter, not the mother."

Slamming the car door with a satisfying thud, I headed for the house, finally breathing in the fresh air of my own truth.

The wake started at two o'clock and lasted until seven. I thought that was going to be way too long. After all, Lily hadn't lived around here since high school. And Crabby couldn't have many friends. Who was going to show up?

Nathan drove us all to the funeral home and Mrs. C sat up front next to him. He was wearing a dark gray suit that made his eyes seem even darker than usual. Or maybe they were getting darker along with his mood: He hadn't even said hello to me when I got into the backseat next to Courtney.

Court whispered to me, "Gramma tried to do my hair in a French braid, but she messed it up. Can you fix it for me?"

She turned her back to me as much as the seat belt would allow, and I took out the sixty-seven bobby pins Mrs. C had sticking up all over the place that still weren't managing to hold much hair in place. I wasn't very skillful at braiding either—Roxanne was the expert—but anybody could do a better job than Courtney's grandmother had done.

Courtney was in dark gray too—a dress with white piping at the neck and hem. She wore white stockings and black leather dress shoes. The outfit made her look so much more grown-up than her usual grubby little-girl clothes. And then it occurred to me that Mrs. C wouldn't have known to pick out clothing this nice. Lily must have bought these things for her children specifically for this occasion. What a terrible chore that must have been!

When I finished with her hair, Courtney turned around and held out her necklace for me to see. It was made of small silver beads and larger blue glass ones.

"Mom made it," Courtney said. "She left it in a box especially for me."

"It's beautiful, Court," I said. "I'm so glad you have

something your mom made for you. You'll have it forever."

"I know," she said, running her fingers back and forth over the strand as though it had magical powers, which, in a way, it did.

The funeral director had put a comfortable chair up near the casket for Mrs. Crosby to sit in. He said "the deceased's children" might want to sit in the chapel's front pew so people could stop to talk to them. But there was also a private room off the chapel, where they could get away from everybody for a while if they wanted to. Mrs. Crosby had made some sandwiches to keep in there, and Mom had sent along a pineapple upside-down cake she'd made the night before. I brought along a bag of apples, thinking it might be easier to get Courtney to gnaw on one of those than to eat a whole sandwich.

I was more than a little scared that the open casket would freak Courtney out. I remembered how weird I'd felt looking at Bunny lying there on lacy pillows in a metal box. I didn't want Court to start screaming like she'd done at the hospital.

But when we walked up to the casket, I was the only one of the three of us to have tears rolling down my face. Nathan stared at his mother in the same zombielike trance he'd been in for days. Courtney looked sad but then perked up and said, "Liz, look at her necklace! It's just like mine!"

Sure enough, Lily's throat was encircled by a necklace

identical to Courtney's. It made me cry harder. How could such a *good* mother die?

Then we sat in the front pew, Courtney in the middle between Nathan and me, and waited.

Lots of people showed up. People who'd gone to school with Lily or remembered her from the riding stable. Tons of old ladies too, who I guess were friends of Mrs. Crosby's, though I never remembered seeing anybody visit her at her house; maybe they just liked going to funerals. At first people poured down the aisles, some of them clutching the hands of their own grown children, many of them teary, all of them stopping to talk to Mrs. Crosby, who sat stiffly in her chair like the Queen Mother receiving guests.

Everybody wanted to meet Nathan and Courtney too, and to tell them stories about knowing Lily when she was young and "full of vinegar." Courtney listened carefully to the tales—she seemed to be memorizing them—but Nathan fidgeted and looked away. As soon as there was a slowdown in the line, we scooted into the back room. Nathan stretched out on a couch and closed his eyes. He hadn't said a word to me all day.

"Courtney, do you want an apple?" I asked. "Or a piece of my mom's upside-down cake?"

But she wasn't listening to me. "I didn't know Mom was a horse rider, did you, Nathan? Did you know she could ride without a saddle? That man said she was a real daredevil!"

"I think I knew it. There are some pictures somewhere." His voice was flat, as if all the emotion had been ironed out of it.

"Pictures? Where?"

"I don't know. Maybe what's-her-name has some."

"*Gramma,* you mean. Don't call her what's-her-name." Courtney glared at him.

"Whatever," he said.

Courtney and I shared an apple and a piece of cake. I made her a cup of tea and she drank some of it.

"We should take Gramma some tea too," Courtney said.

"Oh, we should," I agreed. "That's nice of you, Court, to think about your grandmother. She's having a tough day too."

Nathan gave a sarcastic grunt.

"She is!" I said.

"Since when are you on *her* side," he said.

"Nathan! There aren't any *sides*. What's wrong with you?" I said.

In the same flat voice, he said, "Oh, didn't you hear? My mother died yesterday."

Courtney had just been lifting the tea bag out of the cup. When she heard what Nathan said, she whirled around and threw it at him. It landed on his white shirt.

"Dammit, Courtney!" he said, picking the tea bag off and throwing it on the floor. "Now I've got a big stain on my shirt."

"Too damn bad!" Courtney shot back. "You're a mean jerk!"

Courtney and I went back into the chapel room and left Nathan lying on the couch. Eventually he came back inside, the damp spot on his shirt almost covered by his jacket and tie.

Late in the afternoon Roxanne and Paul showed up, followed by Roxy's mother. Her mom went to talk to Mrs. Crosby, but Roxanne and Paul headed straight for us.

Roxanne grabbed Nathan's hand. "My mom saw it in the paper this morning. I couldn't believe it! Courtney said your mom was sick, but I didn't think she was *this* sick."

He nodded. "She's been sick for a long time."

"Oh, my God," she said, twisting her face into a pained expression.

Paul talked to Nathan then, and Roxanne turned to me. "Did *you* know?"

"For a little while." I glanced at Court. "They didn't want a lot of people to know."

"You could have told *us*! We're not 'a lot of people.' God, Nathan plays basketball with Paul!"

"Rox, it wasn't my decision," I said.

"Still, I can't believe you didn't tell me. I'm your best friend!"

"It's not Liz's fault. They didn't want *me* to know," Courtney said. "'Cause I'm a kid. But my gramma told me anyway."

Roxanne looked guiltily at Courtney, as if she hadn't seen her sitting there before. "Oh, honey, I'm so sorry about your mommy. How's that dog bite? Is it okay?"

Court glanced down at her leg, turning it sideways to see. "I guess. I forgot about it."

"Do you have to stay here all day?" Roxanne asked me. "It's gorgeous weather outside. We're going to the lake."

"I'm staying with Courtney," I said. "In case she needs anything."

Roxanne gave me a crooked smile. "In case Courtney needs anything? Or her brother?" I was pretty sure Nathan heard her. Sometimes I wondered if "best friend" just meant the person who knew you well enough to embarrass you the most.

Courtney stood up and tugged on my hand. "I have to go to the bathroom. Will you come with me?"

Without another word to Roxy we disappeared into the back room. "I thought you just went to the bathroom?" I said.

"That Roxanne can be stupid sometimes," she said. "Let's stay in here until she leaves."

I laughed. "Courtney, you are the smartest nine-year-old I know."

She was already sawing into Mom's cake. "We can have another piece while we wait."

The crowd had dwindled when, at six o'clock, I looked up to see my father walking toward me. I don't know why

I was so surprised. Mom had said she'd called to tell him about Lily's death. I guess in the week since I'd last seen him, I'd started to feel that he was far away from me instead of just in Waverly. Without really thinking about it I stood up and walked into his arms.

"I've missed you so much, Lizzie," he said. "I hate being away from you."

"Me too," I said. "Are you coming home?"

He hesitated. "I need to talk to your mother. We'll see."

"Please come home!" I begged, letting a tear or two slide down my cheek on a well-worn path.

"Don't worry, honey. Things will turn out okay." He kissed my cheek and went to talk to Mrs. Crosby.

"You're lucky," Courtney whispered. "You've got a mom *and* a dad."

What could I say to that? That sometimes I was so mad at them that I wished I didn't? Courtney would think I was terrible, and she'd be right.

"You know what?" I said. "You can share my mom and dad."

She almost smiled. "Like if I was your sister?"

"Sure. I'd love to have you for a sister."

"Me too," she said quietly, laying her head against my arm.

Of course the next person to fly down the aisle was my mother, wearing her Spiritualist glow like radiant good health, which seemed sort of tasteless in a place like this.

"I'm just back," she said, breathing heavily. "I ran from the parking lot, I was in such a hurry to tell you! We spoke to her!" She turned to Nathan. "Your mother is fine! She really is!"

"Christine!" Dad said.

Mom turned around. She obviously hadn't noticed Dad standing there. "Oh, Jack. I didn't expect to see you here."

Courtney was standing now. "What do you mean, you talked to her?" She looked at Nathan, then at her grandmother. "She's dead, isn't she? What do you mean?" There was a flicker of hope in Court's eyes that made me want to choke my mother. What was she thinking?

"She doesn't mean that the way it sounds," I told Courtney.

Mrs. Crosby rose from her chair. "Christine, you been a big help to me these last few weeks, and I appreciate what you done. But I can't have you filling this child with your silly ideas. She's too young to sort out the truth from the ridiculous."

"But it's not ridiculous. If you just let me tell you—"

"I think it would be better if you told us later, when Courtney and Nathan aren't around," Dad said.

And then all hell broke loose. Mom was mad that Dad was telling her what she should and shouldn't do. Nathan was mad that he'd been lumped with Courtney into the category of those too young to know about stuff. Courtney was mad that nobody would explain to her what Mom meant about talking to Lily. Mrs. C was mad that we were all being so noisy at the funeral parlor. And I was mad that my parents couldn't manage to get along for two minutes anymore.

It was finally decided that Mom and Dad and I would go back to our house so Mom could tell us her story. Mrs. C would stay at the funeral home with Nathan and Courtney until seven, and then they'd stop at O'Henry's for dinner. We'd meet again tomorrow for the funeral.

Before we left, I took Courtney aside. "Don't worry about what my mom said. Different people believe different things."

Courtney squeezed my hand. "But I *want* to talk to my mom again."

"I know," I said, hugging her. And really, I would rather have talked to her mother right then than to my own.

Chapter Nineteen

*I*f you'd come with me, you'd know!" Mom insisted. "Lily was there. She was absolutely *there.*"

I perched on the piano bench while Dad paced and Mom ranted. She'd already gone through the story of how Reverend Samuel had sensed "a lovely girl, wearing roses" standing behind her at the service. Maybe Lily had once been a lovely girl, but she was middle-aged and boney by the time I'd met her, and her dress, while flowered, had tulips on it, not roses. I didn't point out either of these things to Mom. I knew she'd have excuses: Reverend Samuel was seeing Lily as she chose to appear to him, and, after all, he was no gardener. How did he know a tulip from a rose?

And when I listened to Mom talk, I almost believed it myself. She said she'd felt Lily's presence walking into the church behind her. Knew Reverend Samuel would see her there. Knew Lily wanted her to tell Nathan and Courtney she wasn't sick anymore. She *knew* these things. Why, she wanted to know, didn't we believe her?

"It's not that I don't believe you," I said. "But it's confusing. I don't know what to believe."

Dad stopped pacing and faced Mom. "Christine, no matter what any of us believe or don't believe, you cannot foist your ideas on those poor children. They're going through enough trauma as it is right now. The idea that their mother is somewhere nearby, behind a cloud or a curtain or something—that other people can *see* her—it's too much to expect them to handle."

"I'm trying to comfort them, Jack. Don't you understand that? It's reassuring to know your beloved is still around you, able to communicate to you."

"It may be a comfort to you, but it'll only upset Nathan and Courtney. Don't you see that? Especially Courtney—she's just a little girl."

"Yes! A little girl who misses her mother!" Mom yelled. And then she started to cry. I knew she was remembering Bunny's death, and I wondered if she would ever get over it. And if *she* couldn't, how could Nathan and Courtney?

Dad put his arms around her, which made me a little hopeful. But Mom pulled away from him quickly and announced, "I suppose we'll never see eye to eye on this."

Dad agreed they probably wouldn't. "Just promise me you won't say anything to the kids," he begged again.

"You know, Nathan is sixteen years old. He's already gone to Singing Creek once. If he wants to go again, I'm not going to *stop* him," Mom said.

Dad sighed deeply. "Fine, but at least don't get the little girl involved. She's too young and impressionable."

"Okay, okay. I won't," Mom said. "Maybe when she's older . . ."

Dad didn't wait around to hear the end of that sentence. He gave my cheek a kiss and left.

What can you say about a funeral? They're all pretty awful, judging from the two I'd been to recently. There's a hole in the ground and everybody knows damn well what's going into it. I sat in the front row next to Courtney, and Mom sat behind us. Dad came too, but he stood in back. There was a minister to say a few prayers, some roses for the family to put on the casket, and lots of tears. In fact, just about everybody was crying, everybody except Nathan.

I wore the same navy blue dress I'd worn to Bunny's funeral seven weeks before. How could only seven weeks have passed when a lifetime's worth of events, great and terrible, had happened since?

Only a handful of people came back to Mrs. Crosby's house afterward—the old stable manager, Mr. Kean and his wife, and two or three of Lily's high school friends. All of Mrs. C's so-called friends vanished. Mrs. Kean had brought a plate of brownies and Mom had ordered a tray of cold cuts from the market. We made coffee and put out the leftover upside-down cake from the day before. Courtney curled into a corner of the couch and sucked on a bottle of root beer as if it were a pacifier.

Mom chatted with Lily's high school friends who she knew too but hadn't kept up with in the years since graduation. I eavesdropped on their conversation, hoping she wouldn't start telling them about Lily's spirit showing up at Singing Creek. Fortunately, the friends mostly wanted to talk about their own lives, their marriages and miseries of the past twenty-five years.

The Keans sat on kitchen chairs and leaned in to talk to Mrs. Crosby.

"This must have been such a shock for you, Eileen," Mr. Kean said.

Mrs. C stared at the crumpled handkerchief in her lap. "Hadn't heard from Lily in twenty years or more. And then she calls me to say she's sick, she wants to come home. All those years and then this. Last I knew, she was hitchhiking up and down the West Coast. Free spirit, she was. *You* know, Carl."

"I do indeed. I'll never forget the sight of Lily Crosby racing around my pasture on that crazy horse of mine." He turned to his wife. "You remember that horse. We called him Commander, and boy, he sure was in command. He wouldn't let anybody else near him, but he ran like a son-of-a-gun for Lily."

Courtney perked up and sat forward. "Do you have any pictures?" she asked him.

"Pictures?" Mr. Kean looked at his wife again. "I don't know that we took many pictures in those days."

"I have some pictures," Mrs. Crosby said. "I'll find 'em for ya later on. When I have my strength back."

Courtney sank back into the couch.

"Will the children stay with you, then?" Mrs. Kean asked, whispering as if we couldn't all hear everything that was said in that small, quiet room.

Mrs. C nodded and sighed. "I told Lily I'd take care of 'em. I don't know quite how we'll manage—I'm not used to havin' children around—but I guess we'll figure it out."

"The Lord will see you through," Mrs. Kean said, her hand on Mrs. C's knee.

"I don't know," Crabby said. "He hasn't helped me out much all these years, but maybe he'll take pity on an old woman. I just hope the next world is a kinder place than this one turned out to be."

Nathan had been hanging around the kitchen, nursing a cup of coffee, but when his grandmother said that, he cracked the cup down onto the table and went out the back door. I followed him.

"Nathan?"

He stomped down the weedy path into an old shed that held a bunch of broken rakes and shovels. When I came in behind him, he whirled on me.

"You don't have to tail after me, Liz. I'm all right!"

"I know. I just . . . We haven't talked much."

"What's to talk about? It's all over."

Did he mean *we* were all over, or was he talking about his mother? I didn't know what to say, and then I guess I said something stupid. "Are you still going to play basketball with Paul's team?"

He stared at me as though he couldn't believe what an idiot I was.

"Who gives a damn about basketball? I was only doing it to pass the time until . . . this. Now that it's over, I'm not sticking around here any longer than I have to."

"But your grandma said—"

"I don't care what she said. She doesn't even want us. At least, she doesn't want me. I'm just another terrible burden the *Lord* has placed on her. Courtney gets along with her okay. She should stay—she's still a kid."

"But . . ." I wanted to tell him I'd be miserable if he left, but I didn't dare. "One good thing" was obviously no longer enough for Nathan. Or maybe he didn't even think of me that way anymore.

Finally I just said, "Courtney will miss you if you go away. How can you leave her now?"

He banged a fist against the wall of the shed and a board splintered. "I'm not leaving *her*! Anyway, Courtney doesn't need me. She'll make friends when school starts. Besides, she's got you for a big sister now. She'll be okay."

"Nathan . . ." I began, but I didn't know how to finish the sentence. There was so much I wanted to say to him, but I didn't know how to say things that were so important. Things like, *Don't leave me* or even, *I need you.* And a funeral didn't seem like the right place to practice my skills.

"I'm going for a walk," he said. "And I don't need any company." He strode quickly down the sidewalk and disappeared around the corner.

I went back inside and ate two brownies. I couldn't wait for the day to be over.

But the rest of the week was not much better. Courtney didn't want to go to the Romanows' with me, and when I talked her into coming over for a piano lesson, she sat slumped over the keys, her wrists limp as cooked lasagna, and couldn't seem to remember anything she'd learned in the past month. Finally I asked her if she wanted to listen to me play, and that seemed to lift her spirits a little bit.

Mom took dinner over to Mrs. Crosby's on Monday night, but Crabby had recovered enough by then to tell her to stop babying them. She said she was perfectly able to cook her own meals and feed her own grandchildren. Meanwhile, Mom hadn't managed to make anything for our own dinner, so I walked down to the farm stand and got corn and boiled it, then made myself a tuna fish sandwich.

Ever since I'd blown up at her in the car, Mom had been keeping her distance from me. She spoke to me, but in an embarrassed way and only when it was absolutely necessary.

On Wednesday evening Roxanne came by, without Paul. We sat on the porch steps and looked across the street.

"I feel awful for them," she said. "Paul said he called Nathan but could hardly get him to talk at all. He won't play basketball anymore either."

"I know. He's in a terrible mood. He says he wants to leave here. He hates living with Crabby."

"Who wouldn't? But he talks to you, doesn't he?"

I shook my head. "Not anymore. I haven't even seen him since the funeral."

"But I thought you were, sort of, together?"

I shrugged. "I don't know. We were, kind of. But now he's different. I don't know what to say to him."

Rox nodded. "Yeah. When somebody dies, I never know what to say to their family. Remember when Katherine Hart's father died a few years ago? I was sitting next to her in math class and it was awful. She always looked like she was going to cry any minute. I was afraid to even borrow a piece of paper from her."

"Can I ask you something weird?" I said. "Do you believe in God?"

Rox didn't even look surprised. "Yeah, most of the time I do," she said.

"What do you think he is? I mean, how do you think of him, or her or whatever?"

She didn't answer me right away, which was unusual in itself for Roxanne. Finally she said, "Well, it sounds strange, but when I think of God, I think of a soft whirring noise—

like a spinning ball of energy—something I can tap into when I need it."

"Wow, that's neat," I said. How had I never known that before? "Is the energy always there?"

She nodded. "I think so. I know it might just be wishful thinking, but it helps me sleep at night."

"My dad thinks God is nature or biology or something," I told her.

"Who knows?" She shrugged. "I guess we all believe whatever makes us feel the best."

As long as we were talking about unanswerable questions, I said, "Why do you think we're alive, anyway? To be happy? Or to help each other? I mean, the whole thing doesn't make much sense when you step back a little and think about it."

"Maybe that's why I don't think about it much," she said. "Except when somebody dies."

"Yeah, me too," I said. "But people keep dying, and now I've got all those big questions stuck in my head."

Roxanne grinned. "You know what my mom says? She was an *X-Files* geek, remember? She says she's just like Fox Mulder. He had this poster over his desk that said, 'I want to believe.' That's my mom. She wants to believe, but she doesn't know what to believe *in*."

"Didn't Agent Mulder believe in aliens?"

"Yeah. I don't think Mom is big on aliens, though. I think mostly she just believes in good-looking FBI agents."

It was nice to be able to laugh again, but that made me

think of Nathan and Courtney. When would they be able to laugh again?

"I'm really worried about Nathan, Rox. He's so *angry* now, he can't say a nice word to anybody. He acts like he hates me. I wish I knew what to do."

"Maybe there's nothing you *can* do right now," she said. "But he'll come around. Nobody can stay mad at you very long, Lizzie."

"What do you mean?"

She shrugged. "I mean, you make me mad sometimes, but I have to get over it because I like you too much."

I was shocked. For some reason it hadn't occurred to me that Roxanne got as aggravated with me as I got with her. "Why do you get mad at me?"

She rolled her eyes. "Well, like, for instance, when you don't tell me about the cool guy who just moved in across the street from you, and then when I meet him, you don't tell me there's this big drama going on in his family. It's like you don't trust me or something."

I was amazed that she knew *why* I hadn't told her. "Well, I couldn't tell you about their mother because—"

"I know, I know. It was a secret from Courtney. But the other thing that bugs me is that you act like we're not best friends anymore just because I have a boyfriend."

"Well, you *are* different now," I said.

"So are you! Anyway, a boyfriend is not the same as a girlfriend, Liz. You need *both*."

"Yeah, I'm figuring that out," I said.

"Anyway, I can never stay mad at you for very long," Roxy said, bumping her shoulder into mine. "You've been my best friend for the past million years. What would I do without you?"

"Thanks," I said, bumping her back. "Maybe if I'd been Nathan's best friend for a million years, he'd talk to me now."

She smirked. "Boys don't need a million years. I saw the way he looked at you. Believe me, he'll be talking to you again soon."

"I don't know, Rox. He's *so* upset. First his mother dies and now he's stuck here with Crabby. He's not thinking about me, he's thinking about escaping from his crappy life."

"Well, you just have to make sure that you're his escape."

By this point I was ready to concede: About certain things, primarily having to do with boys, Roxanne knew best.

"How?" I whined. "I can't follow him around like a faithful puppy."

She thought about it for a minute. "No, you have to be smarter than a puppy. More like a cat. Keep your eye on him, but do it stealthily. Listen hard when he talks to you so you know what his next move will be." She grinned. "And, of course, jump into his lap every chance you get."

"Right. There's no lap for me to jump into at the moment. He doesn't sit still long enough."

"Then stalk him," Roxanne said.

"Rox!"

"Hey, are you in love with him or not?" She waited for

an answer as if she'd asked me a simple yes or no question.

"Geez! I can't just—I mean—I don't—"

"Are. You. In. Love. With. Nathan?" she asked again, staring me right in the eyeballs.

"Yes." I guess it wasn't such a hard question after all.

"That's what I thought," she said. "Now, the way I see it, you aren't going to be in love that many times in your life. I mean, probably more than once, but still, it doesn't happen all that often. It's an important thing, right?"

I nodded, waiting for Roxanne to teach me.

"So, you do whatever you have to do. Stick with him. If he's in a terrible mood and doesn't want to talk, you sit with him. If he wants to walk, you walk. If he wants to talk, you listen. If he wants to be alone, you keep your distance, but you watch. Don't let him get away."

"Oh, Rox, I'm so dumb about boys. What if—"

"You aren't dumb about anything," she said, standing up. "Listen, I have to go. I'm meeting Paul. But remember what I said—do what you have to do."

"Okay." Suddenly I wished she could stay all night and we could whisper and giggle like we used to. I gave her a hug. "Thanks, Roxy."

"You're welcome," she said. "Give me a call if there's a Nathan emergency!"

But Roxanne's good advice couldn't be put into practice unless I actually *saw* Nathan. It wasn't until Friday afternoon that he made an appearance. I was coming back from the Romanows', and there he was on the front porch, beating rag rugs against the porch railing. And when I say beating, I mean beating-the-crap-out-of. Those would be the most dust-free rugs in the county when he got finished.

"Hi," I said, walking over to him. "Where have you been all week?"

"Nowhere. Here. Where else *could* I have been?" His voice was still thick with sarcasm and raw with anger. It made me want to slink back home with a droopy tail, but I remembered what Rox had said: Stick with him no matter what. Cat, not dog.

"Have you seen Paul?" I asked, trying to think of something that might get him talking.

"Nope."

"How's Courtney doing?"

"How do you think?"

"I was hoping she'd come over for another piano lesson this morning, but she didn't."

"Yeah, well, her mother died."

Okay, now he was starting to piss me off. "Nathan! Why are you talking to me like this?"

He shrugged. "Because I'm an asshole, I guess."

"Stop it!"

"Look, Liz, I'm not a normal human being right now, okay? I'm just not. I'm sorry. You should look for somebody else to hang around with."

I ran through Roxanne's advice again. Sit. Talk. Walk. Listen. Jump in lap. I jumped. "I don't want to hang around with anybody else," I said. "You can be an asshole for a while if you need to. I can deal with it."

He chewed his lip and gathered up the rugs to go back inside. "Whatever."

"When am I going to see you again?" I asked him. I wasn't going to let him make a clean getaway.

He turned back. "Maybe tomorrow. I told your mom I'd go with her to that church again."

"What? Did she come over and ask you?" Dad would be angry about that.

"I saw her when I was taking out the trash this morning. She thinks . . . I don't know . . . It sounds crazy, but I have to go and see. If there's any chance . . ."

"Then I'm going too," I said, making up my mind on the spot.

"You don't have to go, just because I am."

"I know I don't *have* to," I said, anger creeping into *my* voice now too. "But if you're going, I'm going. And don't argue with me about it."

His lip twitched the slightest bit and he held one hand out palm forward, giving in. "Fine. Do what you have to do."

Chapter Twenty

I'm feeling the name Jane very strongly. She was a great lover of animals. And her heart," said Running Fox as he clasped his hands across his chest. "It was her heart that gave out, wasn't it?"

A bearded man sitting on one of the saggy couches nodded his head. "Yes, it was."

"She says to tell you—" Running Fox stopped and smiled, but not at any living person. "Yes, she says to tell you 'it's fancy over here.'" The man with the beard nodded, but I wondered if the reading really made any sense to him or if he was just being polite.

Running Fox had done Mom's reading a few minutes before, and it was totally off the mark. It had nothing to do with either Bunny or Lily. Something about an Asian statue and "a gentleman who is splitting hairs." Then he said,

"There's something heavy that you want to lift up. You should go around it instead." Mom smiled and nodded, just like the guy on the couch, but if she understood any of that, I'd be surprised.

Nathan was fidgeting so much our whole pew shook, and his nervousness was infecting me, too. Neither of us had had our readings done yet, though almost everyone else had.

I leaned over and asked him, "Are you okay?"

"I don't know why I came. This is such bull." He said it loud enough that Monica heard it and glared at him.

Just then Running Fox stepped back, and Reverend Samuel came up to do the last few readings. I'd been thinking he wouldn't do any today, or maybe I'd been hoping he wouldn't. His distant stare and weird hand movements gave me the creeps.

Almost immediately his eyes fastened on Nathan. "The boy in the green shirt. May I come to you?"

For a minute I thought Nathan might say no, but when he looked up, his eyes seemed to catch on the preacher's and he whispered, "Yes."

Reverend Samuel's arm shot straight out and his hand started circling. I got goose pimples on the back of my neck as if a cool breeze had blown over me, which was certainly not the case in that stifling room.

"A woman comes through from the generation above you," he said, staring into space as if he were seeing her. "She's tall and thin and has recently passed over."

My God, it was Lily! Wasn't it? Or was I just falling into Reverend Samuel's deep dark eyes again? I grabbed Nathan's hand and tried to glimpse his face, but he had it turned away from me. Was it Lily?

"She says she's sorry, very sorry she had to leave so suddenly. She comes through with a great deal of love."

Mom reached across me and squeezed Nathan's arm, but I don't think he felt either of us touching him. He was stone still.

"I feel she once had a problem with her foot or her ankle," Reverend Samuel continued. "Yes, something that gave her a lot of pain in her life. Is that correct?" Nathan didn't answer, but the reverend kept talking. "She wants you to know her pain is gone now. She's fine. There's a letter *H* or maybe *K*. Perhaps Kate. She asks you not to give your energy to the stress. Do you understand that? She asks you to be patient."

Nathan opened his mouth, but no sound came out. Reverend Samuel looked away from him, for another person to read.

"The lady with the gray hair," he said. "May I come to you?"

But before the woman could speak, Nathan jumped to his feet and started to yell. "No! No, I don't understand it! It makes no sense at all! I don't know what you're talking about, and I don't think *you* know what you're talking about!"

Reverend Samuel turned his head back toward Nathan, although you could tell he didn't want to. "Take it with you. You'll understand it later." He turned back to the gray-haired lady.

"It's bullshit!" Nathan screamed. He was shaking with rage and I tried to get him to sit back down, but he threw off my hands. "You can't prove anything you've said! You're either a fake or a fool, I don't know which. But you're not fooling me!" He pushed past the knees of the man next to him and stalked toward the rear door, then slammed through it.

I stood up to go after him and Mom pulled at my arm. "Don't you dare run after him! I'm embarrassed enough already!"

But I ripped her fingers off me and followed Nathan. I could hear Reverend Samuel reassuring the congregation as I left. "Those who must see to believe don't believe enough to see . . ."

Nathan was already out of sight by the time I got to the parking lot, so I ran up to the highway. Sure enough, there he was, pounding the pavement back toward Tobias.

"Nathan!" I yelled as I ran down the road. "Wait for me!"

"Go on back," he said as I caught up to him. "I don't need you."

"I want to talk to you. What happened?"

He stopped walking and glared at me. "*Nothing* happened, couldn't you tell? That guy is full of shit. He starts out with all this information that sucks you in about "the generation above" and "she comes through with love," and you want to believe him. But what kind of evidence is that? It's vague and meaningless. It could be anybody you want it to be."

"But she said she was sorry to leave you! Doesn't that mean—"

"And who wouldn't want to hear that? Anyway, I thought you didn't buy into this crap."

"You don't either, but you came to see anyway. Just in case." Obviously what we believed and what we secretly hoped were two different things.

"Well, now I've seen. And I don't believe a word of it." He started walking again, but I stayed with him.

"What about the other stuff Reverend Samuel said— about her ankle, and all that?"

"All wrong. She never had a hurt ankle or foot. I don't know anybody named Kate, and Mom would never tell us she's *fine* when she knows we're not. And she wouldn't say, 'Don't give your energy to the stress.' She doesn't talk like some hippie shrink. She didn't, I mean."

"But maybe he's right. Maybe someday that part will make sense to you."

"No, Liz, it won't! Because it's made-up garbage! You don't *really* believe it, do you?"

I shrugged. "Most of the time I don't, but it helps my mom—"

"Well, it doesn't help me! I don't need some ghost mother who 'comes through with love.' I need my real mother, *alive*. I need to see her and touch her and talk to her. I need her to tell me what the hell I'm supposed to do now!" He kicked at a rock and it flew across the field like a football.

I'd never seen anyone so fiercely angry. But I understood what he was saying—those were the things I wanted from my mother too. Of course, I could see her, but for as much as we communicated with each other, she might as well have been a ghost.

We stood there by the side of the road without speaking, Nathan pacing and fuming, me trying to come up with something helpful to say. But there wasn't anything. He was right: Nothing could bring his mother back, and anything less than that was a waste of his time.

A few minutes later Mom's car drove up and stopped. "Get in," she said.

I could tell Nathan didn't want to.

"It's twenty miles back to Tobias," I told him. "You better get in."

Finally he did. It was twenty long, furious, silent miles.

But by the time we dropped Nathan off, Mom didn't seem so mad anymore. She'd morphed back into her miserable self.

"I'm going to lie down a little while," she said as she headed for the stairs.

It was definitely a step backward that she was going to bed

at five thirty in the afternoon. I put on my best upbeat voice and said, "Want me to make some nachos with guacamole for dinner? There's some of that good hot sauce left. . . ."

She shook her head. "Not for me. I'm not hungry."

"Mom, you have to eat!" I insisted.

She turned and looked at me sadly. "You don't believe Bunny comes to talk to me, do you? You don't really believe in Singing Creek at all."

I wished she hadn't come right out and asked me. It wasn't something I wanted to lie about, even if it would make her feel better.

"I guess I don't," I said. "I think it's interesting, but—"

She nodded. "Maybe your father's right. Maybe I *am* nuts."

"No, Dad never said that. He doesn't think that— neither of us do."

But, as usual, she'd stopped listening to me. She pulled herself up the stairs as if the handrail were her lifeline out of a sucking swamp.

I played the hell out of Mozart for a while, just to stop my brain from going over and over all the traumas of the past weeks. Then I made some tea for Mom and me, and had just gotten to her bedroom with it when the phone rang. Since Mom was facedown under the covers, I answered.

It was Courtney, in tears again. "He's gone, Liz! He ran away!"

"Nathan? Are you sure?"

"I'm sure. He took his duffel bag and his favorite CDs and stuff. He ran away!"

"When did he leave?"

"I don't know. When he got back from that church place, he was mad. He told me I should never go there because they were all liars and fakes. Then he went up to his room. That was almost two hours ago. I just went up to get him for dinner and he was gone."

I could hear Mrs. Crosby talking in the background, and then she grabbed the phone from Courtney.

"Hello, is this Christine?" she asked.

"No, it's Liz."

"Well, I'm sorry Courtney bothered you. I imagine Nathan will be coming home soon," she said. Her voice sounded pretty shaky.

I knew "home" wasn't the way Nathan thought of her place. "I don't think he will," I said. "He told me he wanted to leave here. If his stuff is gone, I think Courtney's right."

She let out a deep sigh. "Oh, Lord. I knew he'd be the hard one. I just have no idea . . . I know I'm old-fashioned, but I hoped we could—" Her voice broke.

By this time Mom had rolled over and was sitting up in bed wanting to know what was going on, so I turned the phone over to her while I tried to figure things out. She gasped as Mrs. C told her the story.

"Did he take her car?" I asked Mom. She passed the question along to Mrs. C.

"No," she reported. "He must be on foot, or maybe hitchhiking. She says he doesn't have much money."

The pieces fell into place. I groaned. Not only had I let him get away, I'd made it possible. "Yes, he does. I gave him my babysitting money."

"What?"

"He said he wanted to get something for Courtney—one of those Sweetheart dolls. I gave him a hundred dollars."

"He could have taken a bus," Mom told Mrs. Crosby. "I'm not sure how far you can get on a hundred bucks."

After a few minutes Mom got up and pulled on her clothes again, and we headed across the street to strategize face-to-face.

"Where would he have gone?" Mom wanted to know.

"Home," Courtney said with certainty.

"Courtney thinks he's gone back to Cape Cod," Mrs. C said. "I don't know about that."

I nodded. "She's right. Where *else* would he go?"

"I brought along the bus schedule," Mom said. "If he's headed for Cape Cod, he could have taken a bus from Waverly to Hyannis at six oh five. It gets in at nine fifty."

"What about getting to Wellfleet?" Courtney asked.

Mom studied the schedule. "It looks like he'd have to change buses. There's one that leaves Hyannis at ten fifty and gets into Wellfleet just before midnight."

"What in the world is he gonna do at midnight in that godforsaken town?" Mrs. Crosby wanted to know.

"He has friends there," Courtney said. "We both have friends."

"Well," Mrs. C said, sighing, "I guess we'll just have to wait for him to get in touch with us. I surely would sleep better, though, if I knew for sure where he was."

"Can't we go get him, Gramma? We could get to Hyannis before the bus did and meet him there."

"Oh, Courtney, it'll be dark soon! I'm in no condition to drive to Cape Cod tonight. It's three hours or more from here!"

Courtney wasn't giving up that easily. "But what if he gets there and hides from us? What if he never wants to come back? We need to find him *now*!"

Mom stepped in to comfort her. "Nathan will come back, Courtney. Maybe we should all get some sleep tonight and things will look better in the morning." She didn't sound very sure about that.

"No, they won't!" Court yelled. "He'll just be farther away by then!"

Courtney was right. "Mom, please," I pleaded. "We need to go tonight, or we'll lose him."

Crabby flopped into her chair. "Mercy, I'm so exhausted with alla this."

Mom looked back and forth between Courtney and Mrs. C and me. "I don't know *what* we should do. He'll come back, don't you think? It's a long drive to Hyannis and I . . . I don't want to leave Eileen here alone. She's so frightened."

"I'm not *frightened*, Christine. I'm just worried," Mrs. Crosby corrected her.

I noticed that Mom's eyes were darting around the room as if she were looking for something or someone to turn to, somebody to make this decision for her. This was a woman who had probably wanted to go to bed for a few more weeks, and now she'd been pulled into the middle of an emergency; she looked downright panicked. Forget Mrs. Crosby—it was Mom who was scared. Scared and alone.

I told her I was going to run home to get some chips for Court and me to snack on since none of us had had any dinner. When I got there, I called Dad.

"Nathan got really upset at Singing Creek," I explained. "The preacher told him some stuff that he knew wasn't true and he was *so mad*. He said he wanted his real mother back, not a ghost mother. He wants to get away and stay away, forever. He doesn't want to live with Mrs. Crosby."

"Liz, I feel terrible about this, but what can I do?"

"Go to Hyannis and pick him up at the bus station. Show him that people here *do* care about him, that he has a family here."

Dad sighed. "Poor kid. He must be so confused."

"Mrs. Crosby thinks he'll come back on his own, but he won't. I know it and Courtney does too."

"Well, I imagine you and Courtney know Nathan better than his grandmother does."

"So, we should go right away! The bus gets in at nine

fifty and the one to Wellfleet doesn't leave until ten fifty. We could get there by then, couldn't we?"

"Probably. Did your mother tell you to call me?"

I hesitated a second. "She doesn't know I'm calling."

"Lizzie . . ."

"Dad, she's not doing very well. She went back to bed this afternoon. I don't know what to do."

"Oh, Lizzie, you shouldn't have to deal with this."

"She needs you, Dad, even if she won't admit it. You know she does." There was a deep sigh on the other end of the line. "Please, Dad. We all need you."

He cleared his throat, then said, "I'll be there in twenty minutes."

And he was.

"What are you doing here?" Mom asked when Dad arrived. She had made tea for herself and Mrs. Crosby and they were sipping nervously at the kitchen table while Courtney and I whispered and waited in the living room.

"Lizzie called me. Convinced me we should go to the Cape and look for Nathan."

Courtney ran to him and threw her arms around his belly. "Yes!" she said. "Let's go now!"

Mom glared at me. "I told you I didn't think it was necessary, Liz."

I shook my head. "You know, it's kind of amazing. You can't wait to go talk to your dead mother, but you can't hear a word your living daughter has to say."

Her mouth dropped open. "Liz!"

"It's necessary for me to go look for Nathan, and it's necessary for Courtney to go, and mostly it's necessary for Nathan to know we want him back bad enough to search for him!"

Amazingly enough, Mom stopped arguing then. There were tears glistening in the corners of her eyes, but whether they were for me or Bunny or Nathan or herself, I didn't know. Dad saw them too. He went over and put his hands on her shoulders, which made the water trail down her cheeks.

"But the boy could have gone anywhere," Mrs. C said. "We don't know that he's headed to Cape Cod."

Courtney grabbed hold of Dad's wrist and looked him in the eye. "I know he went to Wellfleet," she said. "He wanted to go home."

I guess Dad believed her. "Well, all we can lose is time and a few dollars' worth of gas," he said. "I'm going before it gets any later. Anybody coming with me?"

"I am!" I said.

"Me too," Court volunteered.

"Courtney, I can't let you go gallivanting all over the place by yourself," Mrs. C said.

"I'm not by myself."

"But if anything happened to you . . . Oh, dammit, I better go too as long as there's room for me."

"I have a minivan," Dad assured her. "There's room for everybody."

I looked at Mom, who was trying to surreptitiously wipe her cheek on her shoulder. "You coming?" I asked her.

She looked at me and then Dad. "This could be a complete waste of time," she said.

Dad nodded. "It could."

She sighed. "There's no real reason for me to go. You and Liz are both so angry with me . . ."

"I'd like you to come, Christine," Dad said. "We can talk in the car."

They looked each other in the eyes for the first time in weeks. "I don't know," she said. "What'll we talk about for three hours?"

"You could talk about how people don't have to agree about every single thing in order to get along with each other," I said.

They were both kind of embarrassed by that, but I didn't care.

Then Courtney piped up, "That's for sure. Me and Gramma don't hardly agree about *nothin'*, but we get along fine!"

"We sure do, don't we?" Mrs. C said. "It's a damn miracle."

Chapter Twenty-One

Mom sat up front with Dad. I could tell they were talking, but I couldn't hear what they said. Mrs. Crosby and Courtney were in the middle seat, both of them fast asleep and snoring by the time we got to the turnpike. I was in the far backseat alone.

I leaned my head against the window and watched the taillights of the cars that passed us. I could almost convince myself we were going on a trip, beginning an adventure—except, who would take Crabby along on their adventure? Still, I had to admit she'd been acting a lot nicer these days than she used to. For example, she called me Liz now instead of "You, Girl!"

And then I started thinking about her—Mrs. Crosby—and how bad she must be feeling. Of course, I'd seen her sniffling for days now, but somehow it hadn't really hit me that she was just as upset over Lily dying as Nathan and Courtney were. Lily was her *daughter*, after all, and even though they didn't get along too well, Mrs. C had been pretty nice to her when she came back to Tobias. I didn't think there was anybody else she would have let move into her house with two kids and all their junk.

I started thinking about how Mom and I had been fighting lately, and I wondered how she'd feel if I died. Would she race over to Singing Creek to see if Reverend Samuel could get in touch with me? I imagined she would, and he'd tell her some things that could be true, if you wanted them to be, and that would make her feel a little better. But if *she* died, I'd just feel terrible that we hadn't gotten along better while she was alive.

I tried to imagine how Bunny would feel about Spiritualism. She was the one who told me about the parables being metaphors and not strictly true. Maybe that was how I could think of Spiritualism, too—as a way to remember people you loved who had died, even if you didn't believe they were really speaking to you through the mediums. I decided to talk to Dad about it when we got back. Maybe he'd be happier thinking of it that way too.

I peered over the second seat into the front. Mom and Dad were still talking. I wished I knew what they were saying. Spinning along through the dark, I kept reminding myself that at least I still *had* two parents, even if they weren't perfect. I decided I'd try to be nicer to Mom, even if she wasn't nicer to me. And I'd be nicer to Dad, too, even if he kept living in Waverly instead of in our house with us.

We pulled over at a rest stop so Courtney and I could go to the bathroom. Dad got coffee for himself and Mom. I noticed the way she smiled at him when he handed it to her. That was a very good sign.

When she saw me looking at her, the smiled flickered, but then it came back on again, like a lightbulb that just needed to be screwed in a little tighter.

"Want a sip of my coffee?" she asked. "It's cinnamon."

I don't like coffee, but I was so glad she'd asked me, I took a little anyway. It wasn't bad.

"Liz," she said, looking at my elbows, then my knees. "I know I'm not as good a mother as Bunny was. I guess I don't . . . I don't know how to be. I'm sorry."

I shrugged and stepped backward, a little light-headed. "It's okay."

"It's not okay," she said, daring to look at my face. "You're more like Bunny was. You can give to other people. You aren't . . . selfish. I admire that, I really do, but I don't know how to do it." Her fingers whisked away a dribble of tears.

"You could probably *learn* how," I said.

"You think?"

I nodded. "You just need some practice."

She sighed. "Well, I guess I'll be getting some. I've asked your father to come back home and he's agreed to."

"Really?" I leaped in the air. "*You* asked *him*?"

"Oh, Liz, I've missed him so much, and I know you have too. Besides, how much more of my cooking could either of us have stood?"

We smiled at each other then, real smiles, and she gave me a quick, one-armed, coffee-holding hug.

"We've both promised to try to be more open-minded about our differences," she said. "We're going to work at this. You'll also be glad to know that Dad has convinced me not to sell the gallery. He says he'll help me with the business end of things so we can get it up and running again. It'll be a family project."

"I'll help too!" I said. "Bunny would be happy about this."

She nodded. "I've been thinking lately that if there was any place on earth I could communicate with my mother without a medium between us, it would be in her gallery. Besides, how could I stand by and see the beautiful space Bunny created being turned into a Gap store or a dentist's office or something?"

There was still one question she hadn't answered. "What about Singing Creek? I mean, maybe you won't need it so much . . ."

Mom swirled the coffee in her cup and stared into it. "I don't know, Liz. Let's take this one step at a time, okay? Dad isn't making any demands on me about Singing Creek. Do you really hate it there so much?"

"No," I admitted. "I even like it when I'm there. It's just later, I feel sort of . . . tricked."

"I won't ask you to go with me if that's how you feel. But try to respect my feelings too. Singing Creek has helped me learn how to live . . . without my mother."

Another tear dripped down her cheek and fell into her Styrofoam cup.

"I know, Mom. I know."

Dad leaned his head out the window. "All aboard for Hyannis, Massachusetts!"

We crawled back into the van and in a few minutes, before I'd even begun to process the fact that my parents were getting back together *and* my mother had actually apologized to me for fifteen years of sloppy parenting, Dad called out, "Hey, everybody! There's the Sagamore Bridge!" I leaned forward to see as much of the silver arch as I could. "As soon as we cross it, we'll be on Cape Cod!"

"Really?" What do you know—I'd gone traveling with my babysitting money, after all.

"When's the last time we were here?" Dad asked.

"I've never been here," I said.

"Is that right? We've never brought you to the Cape? What lousy parents you have!"

Mom sighed. "We used to come pretty regularly before Liz was born. Remember? We ought to plan a trip down here soon. I can't believe Liz has never seen the outer beaches."

"Absolutely," Dad said. "We'll come back as soon as possible. Maybe even later this summer!"

That made me happy on two counts. First of all, they'd both said "we," a lovely little pronoun I'd never paid enough attention to before. And second, a real Cape Cod vacation might actually happen!

"What time is it?" I asked.

"Ten fifteen," Dad said.

"How far to Hyannis?"

"About fifteen or twenty minutes."

"We should make it, then!" Courtney clapped her hands.

"I think so," Dad said. "I just hope he hasn't gotten on the other bus already. I don't want to have to wrestle him off."

"Surely when he sees we've come for him, he won't argue," Mom said. I wasn't at all sure she was right about that.

"He don't like livin' with me," Mrs. Crosby said quietly. I thought she was asleep, but apparently she'd been thinking things over. "To him I'm just an old crab who don't remember what it's like to be young."

I blushed a little when she called herself a crab, but in the dark car nobody could tell.

Mom turned around to talk to her. "It's not your fault, Eileen. He's going through a tough time right now."

"So's Courtney here, but she don't hate me," Mrs. C said. "That Nathan, he's just like his . . ."

She didn't finish her sentence, but the word "mother" hung in the air anyway.

Mom reached her hand back and put it on Mrs. Crosby's knee. "You and Lily made peace with each other. That's so important."

Mrs. C nodded. "Yeah, she let me in there at the end. But, Christine, that was too late. I want my grandson to forgive me *before* I die!"

"Why, what does he have to forgive you for?" Mom asked.

For a minute I thought Crabby wasn't going to answer her, but then she said, very softly, "For not bein' a good mother to his mother. And not bein' a good grandmother to him."

"Oh, Eileen," Mom said sadly, and I knew there was a good chance she was leaking fluids again.

"You're bein' a good gramma to *me*," Courtney said, trying as best she could to curl herself into her grandmother's lap while wearing a seat belt.

"You're *lettin'* me be your gramma," Mrs. C said back. "That reminds me, I found those pictures. Stuck 'em in here so I'd have 'em with me." She fiddled with the clasp on her purse.

"Pictures of Mom riding horses?" Courtney asked, excited.

"Yup. Here they are," she said, handing the snapshots to Court. "I just found these two, but they're pretty good. You can have 'em."

Courtney studied the photos silently in the dim light. I looked over her shoulder, but I couldn't see much.

"You can't see 'em in the dark, honey," Mrs. C said. "Wait'll we get in the light. You don't want to ruin your eyes."

"I love them," Courtney whispered reverently. "I'm glad there's two—one for me and one for Nathan."

By that time Mom had the map book out and was directing Dad which way to turn to find the bus station. "Left here. And it should be . . . There it is!"

It was ten forty. Dad took the first parking space he could find, and we tumbled out of the van as quickly as our cramped legs would allow. Courtney, of course, was in the lead and ran into the station, the pictures of her mother still clutched in her hand.

By the time I got there, she'd already cased the place. "He's not in here. He must have gotten on a bus already!" She wheeled around and headed back out toward the line of buses parked nose-in around the building, like horses at a trough.

There was a driver standing in front of the nearest bus. "Do you know which one goes to Wellfleet?" I asked him.

He pointed across the lot to a big green coach that was just loading on passengers. I scanned the line quickly but not quickly enough. Courtney saw him before I did.

"Nathan!" she screamed, holding up the photos. "Nathan, look what I got!"

She darted across the blacktop lot like a hummingbird

after sugar. I was watching Nathan, waiting for a look of happiness or relief to cross his face. I hoped he'd be glad to see Courtney. And maybe me, too.

Fortunately, Nathan was watching Courtney, and the look on his face was not happiness or relief, but horror. "Courtney!" he screamed, then dropped his duffel bag and ran toward her. I hadn't noticed the bus until then, the one that was backing up right into Nathan's rambunctious little sister.

Mom, Dad, and Mrs. Crosby had caught up to me by then, and the four of us screamed loud enough to wake up the entire town of Hyannis. Nathan grabbed Courtney and dragged her clear of the bus, which was braking by that time, anyway, due to the horrendous racket we were making. When I dared to open my eyes, I saw Nathan and Courtney sprawled on the ground where they'd fallen backward, staring at each other, stunned.

Believe it or not, Mrs. Crosby got to the two of them before anyone else did. She dropped down on her skinny knees and hugged both of them to the front of her saggy dress.

"Oh, Lord, don't ever scare me like that again!" she said, tears streaming down her face. "I just barely found the two a ya—I can't bear to lose ya again!"

"I found Nathan!" Courtney said proudly.

"Found me and practically got me killed all in the same minute," he said. "When are you going to learn to look before you run out into traffic?" His words were angry, but his voice was quiet. He held his sister as if he'd never let her go, and—surprise—he let Mrs. C hold him the same way.

While the rest of us were getting our breath back or picking ourselves up off the blacktop or explaining to the frightened bus driver that nobody had been hurt, Dad went inside the station and made a phone call.

When he came out again, he said, "Okay, I got us rooms in a motel for tonight."

"You did?" Mom was surprised.

"Christine, I'm too exhausted to drive back now. Besides, I think we all need a little vacation."

"Is the motel in Hyannis?" I asked.

"No, it's in Wellfleet."

"Really?" Courtney started jumping up and down. "We get to go back to Wellfleet?"

Nathan wasn't saying much, just looking from one of us to another, as if he couldn't quite believe we were all standing there in front of him at the Hyannis bus station. I managed to get a glimpse of the pictures of his mother that he held in his hand. I wouldn't have recognized her. There she was, a teenage girl, long black hair flying out behind her, riding bareback into her life.

Dad put his arm around Nathan. "This boy went to a lot of trouble to get this far. I don't think we should take him back to Tobias until he gets to visit with his friends in Wellfleet."

"And my friends too!" Courtney demanded.

"Your friends too. We'll get up early tomorrow, have breakfast, and drop you guys off to spend the day with your friends. We'll pick you up in time for dinner, and then go on back home. How does that sound?"

"That's a very kind offer, Jack," Mrs. Crosby said. "I know the children appreciate it."

Courtney gave Dad a tackle-hug around the knees.

Nathan cleared his throat. "I'm sorry you all had to drive all the way down here. But the thing is, I don't want to go back. I want to stay on the Cape." He stared at the ground.

"Well, you can't!" Courtney screamed. "Because I need you at home in Tobias! To keep me from running into the street and stuff!"

"Tobias isn't my home, Courtney."

"I know it don't feel like your home yet," Mrs. C said. "But it *is* your home. It's the home your mother wanted you in."

When Nathan looked up at her, his face was streaked, at last, with tears.

"But I don't belong there," he said.

And then we all started talking to him at once.

"Yes, you do!" Courtney said. "You belong with your family!"

"You already have friends there," I said. "I want you to come back!"

"We'll all be your family," Mom said, and Dad, with an arm around Mom, said, "Our home is yours too."

And, finally, old Crabby herself said, "Please come back, Nathan. I want you to come home." And she sounded like she really meant it.

Nathan didn't say yes or no. He wiped his eyes on his sleeve, followed us to the minivan, and crawled into the far backseat with me for the drive to Wellfleet. I was so glad to have him there beside me, I couldn't stop grinning. I turned my face to the window so he wouldn't see. The road was dark and everybody was too worn out to talk, so Dad got some quiet music on the radio and we all sat there thinking our own thoughts.

Finally Nathan took my hand in his. When I turned to look at him, he whispered, "I'm sorry."

"You don't need to apologize," I said.

"Yeah, I do. I've been acting like a jerk all week," he said. "Plus, I took your money."

I shrugged. "It's okay."

"No, it's not, but I'll pay you back every penny of it."

Sometimes the truth comes to you when you aren't even looking for it. "You know," I said, "I didn't really give you that money so you could buy the doll."

Nathan looked confused. "Sure, you did."

I shook my head. "I gave you the money because . . . because you asked me for it. I wanted to do something for you, and that was what you needed. I would have given it to you if you'd said you wanted to buy yourself vitamins or a cowboy hat or Japanese lessons. I wanted to give it to you."

"Thank you." Nathan leaned over and kissed me, very lightly, then said, "Do you want to come with me tomorrow and meet my friends?"

"Yes," I said. "But only if you'll come back to Tobias with me tomorrow night."

He was quiet, looking out the window again.

"Nathan, you belong in Tobias now," I said. "Don't you see that?"

He let his head fall onto my shoulder then, and I could see his eyelids drooping.

"This has all happened so fast," he said. "I feel like I don't know where I am anymore."

"You're here," I said. "You're with me."

"Yeah," he said, letting his eyes finally close. "That's one good thing."